GREEK GOLD

A NOVEL IN TWO PARTS

by Susan Barrett

For Peter,
my most important reader,
in gratitude for years of patient support

Greek Gold is the story of a wartime hero and the daughter he never knew. In Part One, Alex, a newly married SOE agent, is dropped into German-occupied northern Greece in 1943. Badly hurt on landing, separated from supplies and his wireless operator, he gets in with the 'wrong' band of resistance fighters. His second mistake is to fall in love with a Rumanian-Greek, Ileana. Within a couple of months, he is dead. In Part Two, his daughter Helen, born after he was killed and now a widow herself, visits the scene of his death, hoping to find out more about his heroic action. Slowly she learns the truth from the villagers, in the company of newly-met Heinrich, a German plant collector, lecturer and widower. Helen revises the picture of her father. He was not the hero she thought he was but his all-too-human failings have brought him alive for her.

Even gold contains impurities.

Author's note

This is a work of fiction and any resemblance to anyone, living or dead, is unintentional. However, the background – history and landscape – is rooted in life experience. A reader wouldn't be able to find the places nor meet the people in reality, but you might feel you had come close.

PART ONE
1943

I CHAPTER ONE

The worst phase of a jump, Alex found, lasted no more than five seconds. You've hurled yourself into the dark abyss. There is no return. You trust your 'chute will open. They don't always. Many tales are passed around to frighten first-timers. Oh, but *you'll* be all right, they say, after a realistic description of a failure. Alex blocked his mind to the tales. As a rule, he was confident that things would turn out all right. But over the moonlit mountain plateau in northern Greece, at the moment when he jumped out into nothingness, his meagre supply of trust melted away, leaving only a liquid feeling in the pit of his stomach. He couldn't remember if he'd started counting or not. Was it too soon to pull the rip cord? Was he clear of the plane? His gloved fingers were too clumsy, yet – thank his lucky stars! -the parachute billowed open above him. His plummet to earth became a gentle descent. His breathing steadied and, as often happened on drops, euphoria set in. He drifted earthwards through the night sky. Moonlight lay in pools on the ground beneath him; black, jagged shapes hinted at cliffs and chasms. Alex tried to make sense of the terrain below, hoping to match it with the contour map he'd studied in Cairo.

Dandelion puffs of parachutes floated to earth below and behind him. Alex, twisting in his harness, counted five. These would be Lenny, his radio equipment and whatever Ordnance had provided to keep the two of them alive and the resistance group on side: food, drink, clothing, ammunition, boots and gold guinea coins. Alec looked ahead and saw, with a jolt of alarm, that he was drifting towards what looked like an edge. An edge where there should be none. Coming towards him fast was a sudden absence of ground. It was as though a deep chunk had been gouged out of the mountain. A disused quarry? Surely not, at this --- but he had no time to complete the thought. His boots were skittering on scree; he was being pelted with rocks. One caught him on the side of his head. Another got the base of his skull. He felt no pain; simply extreme indignation.

He was next aware of dizzy discomfort, an intense chill, and a change in the quality of light. All was still and silent. Taking stock of the situation, he realised that his feeling of nausea meant he'd been knocked out. He told himself the facts as he remembered them. He'd been on a plane for a night drop. Not into France. Somewhere else. He'd recall where in a moment. It was no longer night, yet it wasn't fully day. There was a chill greyness around and above him, which seemed to emanate from the rocks in his immediate view. He made a mental check of his body. He was lying in an awkward position, with one foot wedged in a crevice, trapped by a boulder the size of an Austin 7. This foot, his right, was the source of one of the many points of pain he could identify. Another lay deep within his right shoulder. He was lying on his side in a steep gully; it looked like a dried-up watercourse. He could imagine cataracts of water cascading over the ledge where he lay. Smooth rock faces rose on either side, carved out over eons of time by snowmelt and winter deluges. Thin, white rope lay around and about him and came from somewhere behind and above his head. Beyond the boulder that trapped his foot lay other boulders which dropped away into space. On the far side of this darkness was a cliff where pinnacles of rock emerging from trees were lit at their topmost edge by sunlight.

With his mind now working less sluggishly, he recalled jumping from the plane. He heard an urgent voice: *Go, go.* Lenny had gone first. Then the bundles of equipment. There'd been a miscalculation. The pilot overshot the dropping ground. He should have gone around a second time but Alex heard another *go, go.* He'd jumped. In Cairo someone had casually mentioned a gorge but in terms that placed it far, far away from the plateau. It was not far away at all. From a careful study of his surroundings, he reckoned he'd fallen into a deep gully which plunged down one precipitous side of the gorge.

Conscious of the need to be unseen and unheard in this foreign territory, he clamped his mouth shut against the forceful flow of four-lettered words needing expression. Silently he swore at the men in the Cairo HQ, idiots one and all with their inaccurate maps and useless information. He swore at himself for failing to write that last letter to Joan. And yes, it could be his last. She would never know exactly what had become of him. There'd just be a brief telegram, delivered to the door. His breath caught in his throat. Who was going to find him, in this godforsaken terrain?

He heard a chorus of voices. *"What a pickle."* *"Now look what you've done."* *"No good crying over spilt milk."* The admonishing voices came from a period in his childhood he did not wish to remember. He could recognise his father's voice saying something about valour. Was caution the better part of valour? Or some other quality lost in the mists of memory? *"Time spent in reconnaissance is seldom wasted."* Whoever said that had not landed in a steep ravine in a war-torn country. *"Down the karzi into deep shit."* That laconic voice belonged to Lenny, his wireless operator.

Some sort of order was returning to the thoughts crowding around his aching skull. Despite an overpowering desire to go to sleep, he summoned a series of scenes from his recent past: sailors and kit bags packed into a train corridor; his own seat in a compartment, wedged between a chain-smoking, sharply-suited man and an elderly woman who held a wicker basket on her lap. Pitiful mewling came from the basket. Joan ran towards him, down the garden path of Colebrook Farm. The latch on the gate stuck and they both fumbled over it, laughing. Her mother gave him a huge helping of rhubarb pie and heaped dollops of clotted cream on top of it. *We need to build up your strength.* Alex found the experience of being fussed over both welcome and alarming. Joan and he made love in the wood at the top of the hill because the double bed brought into her childhood bedroom creaked too loudly. A fern was caught in her hair, a green frond tangled in one of her corkscrew curls. She longed for straight hair. "At least," she'd said to him on their wedding night, "it's straight down there." She was a matter of fact lover. He put it down to her farming background.

With an effort, he brought his mind back from his last leave and focused on a picture of the Cairo briefing room. There was a map pinned to a board propped on an easel. It showed the area of the mountain where they would be dropped.

The pattern of contours made him think of a lion couchant, like one of those gleaming black shapes in Trafalgar Square; head held aloft, long back ending in rounded haunches. The dropping zone was a plateau on the lion's back. The pilot was to approach from the south-east and circle the lion's head to the north-east, looking out for signals from the ground. Then, flying due south, he would give the order for the drop over the lion's long back. This would allow plenty of time before the plateau ended in a jumble of forested hills which hid several villages, the centre of resistance in the region. Alex, the last to jump, must have landed, not on the lion's back, but somewhere at the head end, where the rivulets were carved in the lion's mane. It was as though the pilot had read the map the wrong way around. Could that possibly be the case? Whatever had happened, he would have to climb back up to the plateau and find Lenny.

Climb! Could he move at all? He heard his own gasp of pain as he attempted to wiggle his foot out of the crevice. It was jammed in tight. The first thing to do, then, was to shift the boulder under which his foot was trapped. It took several agonising minutes to get himself into a sitting position where he could lay both hands on the boulder and start to push. He'd probably broken his collar bone. That was pain enough but it wouldn't impede his ability to climb and walk. It simply made it harder to use his right arm with any strength. He shuffled nearer the boulder on his butt and twisted himself around to get his left shoulder and a portion of his back against it. For a while he pushed and rested alternately. He recalled reading a story about someone who'd been stuck in the same way; that particular hero had used a blunt penknife to cut off his foot to free himself. Alex had a penknife in a top pocket of his battledress. Its blade was not blunt but he didn't feel like a hero. On the contrary, he experienced the hollow feeling he recognised from prep school days when he'd been left in the school's gothic doorway to watch his father drive away in the black Daimler with his new wife. Tears welled into his eyes.

BUT. He bloody well would not feel sorry for himself. Hell, he'd barely begun his battle with the boulder. All he needed was a short rest.

"*A spot of bother,*" Alex heard. He was back in London. The words came from the man behind the desk.

Alex could see the outline of his head, a bald pate with fuzzy clumps over each ear, thrown into relief by a chink of daylight from the boarded-up window. Two panels, which looked as though they'd been ripped from the side of a crate, didn't quite meet in the middle. A shoddy job, thought Alex; then he corrected himself. A hasty job. The windows on the Baker Street side of the building had only been shattered yesterday.

The room was blue with tobacco smoke. It smelt like Gold Flake. He could do with a smoke himself.

"In Greece," the outlined head continued.

Alex wished he could see the officer's features more clearly. He needed to judge the nature of the man, never having met Major Blewitt before. He'd heard all the jokes, though. The poor bloke, fresh from the Cairo office, had an unfortunately apt name, taking into account the number of mess-ups that had apparently happened out there. All to do with the *Balkans*.

"In the north-west corner of the mainland. The Pindos mountains."

Alex had decided before entering the office that this was a mission he'd refuse. France was the country he knew. He spoke French. If he worked it right, he should get the long leave due to him before another drop into the Auvergne where he'd carved out a relatively safe niche.

"You read Classics at Cambridge."

"Yes, but -"

Blewitt cut in. "You'll get by. The *alpha beta* hasn't changed. Pronunciation's fiendish though, not as we were taught. I visited Greece in the early 30s. Ever been yourself?" It wasn't really a question. Blewitt would already know everything he needed to know about Alex Pritchard, Captain R.E.

He shook his head, feeling resigned.

"You'll be dropped in the northern Pindos, near the Albanian border. Far from the madding crowd." Blewitt smiled at him, in a way that said 'rather you than me.'

Ignorance of Greece and its modern language was unlikely to save him from this assignment. There'd be no need to blend with the local civilian population as they had to do in France. He'd be himself, a British officer in uniform, sharing a cave with a band of lawless brigands. He'd learnt this much from the fellow who'd sent him in to see Blewitt. Recently returned from Greece, he'd described being holed up in mountain hide-outs in bitterly cold weather, subsisting on dry rusks and the occasional billy goat stew. He'd been part of a team which had blown up a railway viaduct. Alex had felt a surge of excitement on hearing this. Nothing like a good big bang or two, so long as you get away fast enough. But he'd rather do this in France.

Blewitt was still speaking. "Right up your street, I believe."

Alex took this in. His trek through Kyrgyzstan was no doubt in his file, perhaps even details of the rather messy incident at the Kara-Buura pass. He might have to accept Greece. These people always have a hold over you.

But he would try to get out of it. "My wife's expecting," he said.

"Jolly good," said the major, pushing a folder across the desk. "Have a read of this and report back at 14 hundred hours tomorrow."

Alex leant forward in his chair. "I'm sorry, sir. I really have to turn this one down. My wife's due any moment." He was within his rights. His voice was mild but firm. It wasn't far from the truth. Joan might well be expecting after his forthcoming leave.

"I'm sorry, too," said Blewitt, getting to his feet and coming around the desk. His ironical tone of voice milked the words of any sympathy. In the light of a desk lamp, oversized teeth glinted under the clipped hedge of moustache. He looked as though he was enjoying himself. "Wives. Babies. They go on all the time." He seized the folder from the desk. The action filled his voice with sudden energy. He struck the folder with the side of his fist. "*This* doesn't go on all the time." Another thump. "*This* is the war." A final thump. "*This* takes priority."

Alex found himself being walked towards the door, Major Blewitt's arm around his shoulders. There was talk of the need for speed. Alex would learn why. It was all in the file. More gen would be on offer the next afternoon. With a parting slap on his back, Alex was propelled from the room. In the corridor outside, he pulled a packet of Gauloises from his pocket. Two left. Odd, how shaky his knees felt.

Shaky knees, yes, but mainly dry mouth. The place where he lay was now in full sun. Sweat poured down his face. His battledress prickled his arms and legs. His pistol was missing from its holster on his waistband, as was his water flask. He did have the emergency tin, the size of a pack of playing cards, in his lefthand top pocket. There was a square of chocolate in it, beside the death pill. He would take neither, that was absolutely clear. The chocolate was not yet necessary and would only wake his hunger. As for the other, he was by no means ready for *that*. With renewed vigour, he put all his weight and strength behind the boulder, lifting and pushing as best he could at the same time. He felt it wobble. Over the next half-hour he persevered, making the boulder wobble briefly before it settled back into position over the crevice. Then suddenly he got it past the critical stage. It teetered for a second and then rolled forward and down the watercourse, setting off an avalanche of stones. Alex could hear it crashing down the mountainside. He flexed his ankle and a searing pain shot up his leg. This boded ill for his clamber up and out of the ravine. But he was free. He crawled to the edge of the rocky shelf and looked down. At first it was hard to take in the sight which greeted him. The drop was vertiginous: the narrow gully fell away for a good distance before it disappeared under overhanging trees. A cloud of dust was rising above the tree tops. By the sound of it, rivulets of stones were still falling in the wake of the boulder. The far side of the gorge was closer than he'd at first thought; perhaps only half a mile away. By looking directly across, he could gauge his own position. He reckoned he'd tumbled down about a fifth of the height of the gorge; probably about 100 meters. It wouldn't take long to climb back up the gully to the plateau. Lenny and the band of *andartes* would be searching for him.

For the first time since coming to consciousness, he thought to look at his watch. The position of the sun lined up between twelve o'clock and the hour hand would give him south. He got himself into a halfway comfortable sitting position. With a sharp burst of pain in his right shoulder, he pushed back the sleeve of his jacket on his left wrist. The glass covering the watch face was shattered; the thin black hands were skewed. Although he held the watch to his ear, he knew it was useless to expect to hear a tick. In a surge of anger at his misfortune, he undid the silver buckle of the leather strap and was set to hurl his watch into space when shoulder pain stopped the movement. He changed hands but his left arm had little strength. The watch fell feebly, just twenty feet below on another shelf of rock. Alex regarded it with dismay. He'd lost the means of gauging his compass bearings. Worse than that, Joan had given the watch to him as a wedding present.

This had been an ill-fated mission from the start. Careful, Alex warned himself. He must keep his mind on the task in hand.

From the scraps of information he could recall from the Cairo briefing, the gorge - which had STUPIDLY not been considered to be within the dropping zone, when it so BLOODY obviously was! - scored the mountain in a south-west to north-east direction. He must be facing north-west. It was late August. The sun was strong, the heat intense. If he'd been dropped in the winter, he'd have snow to slake his thirst. His head was pounding. He was in a lift going down, but in a strange, whirligig way which made him feel very sick.

He must have lost consciousness again because when next he was aware of his surroundings, the sun was just two fingers' width above the skyline on the opposite side of the gorge. A whole day had passed! Why hadn't Lenny and the group of *andartes* hunted for him? Couldn't they have thought to search the gully? This was a fuck-up. Of major proportions.

For a moment, he sank into a familiar pattern: a sequence of thoughts which he knew of old. *Give up. It's no good. No-one will help you. You're on your own.* As always, he recognised the feeling of abandonment that lay behind all the thoughts. This had to be dealt with before it succeeded in pulling him into a darkness from which he'd find no escape. *Get a grip*, he told himself. *Fast.*

His resting place in the gully was now in shade. The loss of the sun's heat helped him stir into action. With some difficulty he got himself upright, his weight on his left foot. He had a target in mind. The parachute. That was the first thing to deal with. Set yourself obtainable targets. Don't lose sleep over long-term aims which may prove impossible to achieve. He would make a sling for his arm out of parachute silk, and a bandage for his ankle.

All he had to do right now was to reach the parachute, not far above his present level. As far as he could judge from his immediate position, the ravine was formed like a staircase, with stairs of uneven heights. The stair he had to climb was head-height, so six foot three or so. Not a problem, in the normal course of events. But this was not a normal event. It could be terminal. Normal, terminal. He was slipping into his train journey occupation, making up rhymes to the rhythm of the engine. Joan passed train journeys by riding her horse, jumping over the hedges as they sped past the train's windows. Here's a good gap coming up – jump now, she'd say. They'd only had two shared train journeys in the pitifully short time they'd been married.

Tears pricked at the corners of his eyes. *Missing in action.* He imagined a telegraph boy cycling from the Pinhoe Post Office to the farm. Joan would collapse in a heap. Or would she? She was such a matter-of-fact person. She'd probably become engaged to someone local in no time at all.

This gave him fresh strength. He would not die! In any case, there'd be many better places for this sad event than a ravine where no-one would find his body for days, if at all. Think, he told himself. *Think.*

The white rope that lay entangled around his body led from the harness still on his back to the parachute. He could pull the parachute down to his level, rather than climb up to get it. Alex smiled wryly to himself. Sensible thoughts were being extremely hard to bring to mind and hold there. The mental effort was as hard as the physical effort required to carry out the thought. Eventually, he succeeded in hauling the parachute down to lie in folds of white silk at his feet. With his penknife, he cut out a number of long strips. Then he removed the boot and sock from his right foot and inspected his ankle. It was grossly swollen and the colour of ripe plums. Just a sprain, he told himself. All it needs is support. He wrapped three long strips of parachute silk around his ankle and ripped an eight inch parting in one end of the fourth strip. This gave him two strands to tie in a knot to secure the fourth layer, making a firm, thick bandage. He stood up and tested how much weight he could put on his foot. Perhaps it was not quite as painful as he'd feared. Now he could make himself a sling for his right arm. He'd be up and out of this damned ravine in no time at all. *I'll be home before you know it*, he told Joan.

His confident words mocked him as he struggled to scramble up the ravine, only to find that the shelf above was bounded on all sides by sheer rockface, save for the one he climbed. Snow melt over millennia had hollowed out a smooth funnel without footholds. The only way out of his predicament was downwards. The sooner he attempted that before nightfall, the better. Negotiating his way carefully in a crabwise, half-crouching, half sitting position, he began the long descent, favouring his good, left leg as much as possible. He paused every now and again to gauge his progress by what he could see of the opposite side of the gorge, until trees crowded in on either side and formed a green-leafed archway overhead, hiding any view. When he reckoned he was within two hundred feet of the point where the ravine must meet the riverbed of the gorge, he stopped for a moment to listen. A faint tinkling sound had penetrated his intense concentration. He strained to identify the sound. Bells? A waterfall? The thought of slaking his thirst drew him onwards. In his eagerness to reach water, he put all his weight on the next boulder without first testing its stability. It gave way beneath his foot, and he fell onto his back while the boulder crashed forwards to bounce out of sight below. A few seconds later, he heard a faint thud, followed by the spattering noise of falling stones and an outbreak of distant bleating with a crescendo in the musical, tinkling sound. He guessed a flock of goats, with bells around their necks, was scrambling for safety. He recalled scraps of information. *Sheep and shepherds on the high mountain plateau. Goats and goatherds near villages in the foothills. Beware of the villagers, except for the ones you trust.* How a lost newcomer works out which villagers to trust was a question not covered by Cairo. Nor had they foreseen a landing in a deep ravine.

The final stretch of descent to the gorge floor became a bumpy toboggan slide which brought him to rest on a patch of shingle beside what must be swirling water in wintertime but was now a dry, rocky riverbed. There was no sign of goats – although he could hear their bells coming in faint arpeggios from further down the gorge to the north-east. He sat listening intently until he could hear nothing but silence. When he was at last satisfied that he was far from any habitation, he lay back on the shingle in a position that, to a small degree, relieved the pains in his shoulder and ankle. It was twenty four hours since he and Lenny had flown out of Cairo. Now he was alone, without any means of contact.

Yet he was alive and for the moment safe. He felt protected by the immense height of the gorge's walls. An intermittent current of air carried the scent of herbs. Above him spread the night sky, brimming with stars. With a trick of his mind, he could turn the landscape upside down and see the sky as water sparkling at the bottom of a well. He was drifting into waves of sleep when the resounding silence was broken by a soft, two-toned call from a distant crag. Alex tensed in immediate response. The call was softly echoed further down the valley.

He lay rigid for a good while before he trusted his guess: his only companions in the gorge were owls.

I CHAPTER TWO

Alex woke with the strong conviction he was being watched. He sat up cautiously, taking care to minimise the sudden jabs of pain his movements caused. As far as he could tell from a slow and careful scan of his surroundings, he was alone – or, just as doubtfully alone as he'd felt before falling asleep sometime around dawn. Now, although he was still in deep shadow, the sun was up, picking out the sharp edges of the gorge's high cliffs with pinkish-golden light. How steep and narrow were the sides of the gorge! What a disastrous drop he'd made! What would be going through Lenny's mind? Where was he? Had he got a search party out? Would he guess Alex was injured? Would he – or the local resistance - think of looking in the gorge? Whatever was in Lenny's mind, he, Alex, must do his best to find him, rather than wait to be found.

His brain was working better than it had done the day before and he was able to match his present surroundings with information learnt in Cairo. The ravine – he now thought of it as *his* ravine - scored a long, deep cleft from the height of the plateau, the scene of the mishandled drop, to the floor of the gorge where he now sat. If he followed the gorge upwards in a southerly direction, he'd be led to its origin in the lower slopes of the mountain. The resistance group that he and Lenny were to join operated from a base in this region, supported by four villages, called just that, Tesserahori. They lay close to each other in thick-woods. But he could more quickly and easily reach another village which also supported the resistance, called Glikopigi. It was separated from the four by the bulk of the mountain. He could picture the map. If he headed northwards, down the gorge, he'd reach a spring, the source of a river that flowed north into Albania. A few kilometres further on from the source, he'd find the mule track that led from the distant main road, through the foothills of the mountain, across a bridge, to end finally in Glikopigi, higher and within a curve of mountainside beneath what he'd imagined as the lion's head. Taking this route would be more dangerous. It would take him nearer the main road, and German troops. On the other hand, he'd reach water more quickly.

Red-hot pains shot up his calf the moment he put any weight on his foot. He needed a stick. Hunting among the rocks at the foot of the ravine, he found a suitable length of stout hazel-wood. Despite the pains in his right shoulder – not nearly so acute as those in his ankle, *look on the bright side* - he trimmed away any offshoots with his penknife and created a notch for his thumb at one end. Satisfied with the stick's support, he set off. Action. A target. He felt a surge of optimism. Was it the clarity of light, the sun now warming his face, the tangy freshness of the air? What made him feel – yes, positively cheerful. He'd always liked long hikes on his own. And the landscape was exhilarating.

Haphazard goat trails were easy enough to follow as they led up and down and around rocky promontories, sometimes on one side of the gorge, sometimes the other. As he struggled onwards, he rehearsed his next moves. When he reached the village, he would risk a direct approach. How could anyone, living in a village called Glikopigi, Sweet Spring, be anything other than the source of kindness and delight? In any case, Cairo had assured him that the Germans rarely left the main road, over 20 kilometres away. Only mule tracks connected the villages. And two telephones, one in Glikopigi, one in Tesserahori. News of the drop would have spread rapidly. The right people would know where he was.

Alex imagined a bowl of hot water and some soap. He would be able to bathe his foot, he'd be given a proper bandage, it would be bound up securely; the same treatment for his shoulder, with a fresh sling; he'd be given food: hearty soup, hunks of rough bread, cheese, the sort of food he was given in the Ardennes. Maybe not such delicious country sausages as in France, but certainly goat's cheese. He could fill a glass as many times as necessary with clear, spring water to quench ... but before he completed this welcome thought, a violent commotion erupted ahead. Barking, a scattering of stones, more barking – and two ferocious looking dogs were skidding down a scree slope on the far side of the gorge towards him. Alex looked around for a large stone to hurl at them, should they leap across the intervening rocks. But he couldn't hold and throw a stone, with one arm in a sling, the other leaning on his hazel-wood stick. He was relieved to see a figure some distance above the dogs: their owner, without a doubt. A goatherd. He'd heard goat-bells yesterday. The dogs were in a frenzy of excitement on the opposite bank, teeth bared, the white hair on their backs bristling, but – as yet – just madly circling, not leaping across.

Call them off, shouted Alex, knowing full well that his English words were useless even if they could be heard, yet unable to summon any Greek. The goatherd began to descend the scree slowly and Alex realised, with a little shock, that this was a young woman. She held her long, brown skirt bunched up in one hand to make her descent easier. He watched her move steadily and nimbly down the scree. As she drew near, the dogs went silent and skulked away behind her, up the slope. The girl had not uttered a word of command. Nor did she call anything to Alex in the way of a greeting. She simply sat down on a boulder, ten yards or so away, on the opposite bank. It was as though she was preparing herself for some kind of entertainment from which she'd stay aloof, with as little likelihood of conversation as between audience and actor. Was he to be her entertainment? Or was it fright or caution that kept her silent? After all, he was in khaki summer kit, obviously a soldier.

"English!" he called. "Inglezi!"

She tilted her head sideways, tucking in her chin. This was the Greek way of agreeing, Alex had been taught. So she understood he wasn't a German.

"Glikopigi?" He pointed down the gorge. "How far?" He raised three fingers of his left hand, then all five.

The girl regarded him but said nothing.

"Water?" Alex mimicked the act of drinking.

The girl repeated the tilted-tucking motion of her head and pointed up the mountainside behind her. The dogs were just visible, lying in a segment of shadow at the foot of a high cliff.

He wasn't going to climb up there for water. He pointed down the gorge. "Water?"

The girl swung her arms in a criss-cross way, one over the other, palms to the earth. A clear negative. She appeared anxious he should not continue down the gorge. She imitated the firing of a gun; then more criss-cross movements, followed by both hands up in the air, pushing against the view down the gorge.

His classical Greek was coming back to him as he watched her. He spliced a sentence together with the fragments of present-day demotic mugged up before the mission. He called across something that probably sounded as quaint to her as it would in English: "Sustenance is needed. I am broken and empty."

Whatever she understood from this, it led to more vigorous sign language. He was to cross over the dry, boulder-strewn riverbed to her side. This he did, with great difficulty. Once across, he understood from the girl he was to come close to the boulder where she sat. He obeyed. She told him to sit at her feet on the ground. He smiled wryly. She was behaving like a princess on a throne; he was her father's subject. Yet she was so young, so small! Fifteen perhaps?

She regarded him solemnly. Then she touched her throat and tapped both ears. She seemed to expect some response from him. Her perfectly arched eyebrows were raised above questioning brown eyes. High cheekbones. Little bosoms beneath a faded, embroidered bodice. Skirt bunched up around brown legs. *Bare feet!* On this scree.

The sun was beating straight down. He was hot. Dizzy, in fact. The girl was a gypsy princess, casting a spell on him. Her eyes, like her hair, shone a glossy, dark brown that was almost black. The skin of her face, like her arms and legs, had the quality and colour of polished applewood. Her mouth was twisting in strange movements. Guttural sounds were emerging. The contrast between the awkward sounds and the beauty of the girl caught him unawares. In his weakened state, tears of sympathy filmed his eyes. He gazed at her, longing for her to stop straining. He understood well enough. It was the sadness of it that caught him. This gorgeous young creature, so full of grace, who could model for a Parisian fashion house, was dumb.

Yet her expression was animated. Her hands flew about, giving urgent messages. After some repetitions, he understood. There were Germans further down the gorge. "In Glikopigi?" he asked.

She raised her chin and closed her eyes. No. She pointed up and away from the gorge to the north-east. Glikopigi was high up on the mountainside, way over there. She clasped her hands and rocked her arms. Safe. She would show him the *safe* way to the *safe* village. She pointed to his head, his arm, his foot. First, he must recover from his wounds. Then she mopped her brow. There was something comical about the girl's miming. A scrap of memory came fleetingly to mind: a game of dumb crambo at Christmastime, when his mother was still alive. He smiled at the girl. Was she fourteen? he asked in Greek. Sixteen?

She regarded him with surprise, before her lips parted and her mouth spread in a wide smile. She raised both her hands skywards, then let them drop into her lap, in a gesture of complete despair. Yes, he understood. They could only communicate with signs. He lay his good hand on his chest and bowed his head in acceptance. She smiled some more. Her teeth were small, even and white – unusually so, he thought, remembering the broken, skewed and yellowed teeth of country people he'd met in French villages. The girl was laughing; it was more an upheaval in her shoulders and chest than a sound. She brought a long lock of hair forward from its position behind an ear and ran it through her mouth. She ducked her head and looked up at him, a deeper colour coming to her cheeks. Then she began signing again, faster than ever.

An involuntary shiver went through him. It felt like an echo of recent sensations: dropping from the plane, falling into the ravine, getting knocked out, losing consciousness. Would meeting this girl be similarly disastrous? Certainly something momentous was happening; something that he'd have to think about and label when he had the chance. For the moment, he was concentrating on the girl's sign language. He understood that she was going to take him up the scree slope to her home. He also understood, when they began the climb, how weak and feverish he was. She had to half-carry him, one arm around his waist, his good arm around her shoulders. Although she was a slip of a thing, her lithe body felt wonderfully strong beneath his dragging weight. Even so, they kept resting to catch their breath on their zigzag path upwards.

When they eventually staggered to a halt, he saw he was by a cave in the mountainside. It lay at the back of a wide shelf of rock, overhung with ivy. He sat down heavily on a makeshift bench by the entrance: a plank of wood resting on two rusted, rectangular, tin cans. The girl disappeared inside the cave and re-appeared almost at once carrying a glass and an army canteen of water. She refilled the glass three times before he felt he'd had enough. Then she led him inside the cave and indicated a low bed in a dark recess. He fell on it with such relief that he had no thought for his boots until he realised they were being unlaced and eased off his feet by the girl. Next, she tucked a rough blanket around his body. Being looked after was a strange sensation which made his breath come in spasmodic waves. Ridiculously close to childish tears, he lay in a state veering between high tension and utter collapse until he was overcome by a nauseous sleep.

For a puzzling length of time, he struggled in and out of nightmares involving accidents: he was in a vehicle – a car, a train, a plane - which was about to crash, or had crashed. He needed to send urgent messages and he had no means of doing so. He was letting someone down; he didn't know who this person was, nor what he'd done or failed to do. When he came briefly to consciousness, he knew his dreams were close to what had really happened, but he hadn't the energy to work it out. Sleep was what he needed.

Sometimes he woke to candlelight flickering on the rocky ceiling above his head. Other times the mouth of the cave was filled with bright sunlight. The girl was often beside him, bathing his forehead with a damp cloth, or holding a cup of warm goat's milk to his lips. She'd made a new sling for his arm from a blue and white striped piece of cotton. His head was now bandaged in the same material; he could see a frayed edge above his left eye. He felt a nagging pain on that side of his forehead and at the base of his skull. One day, he told himself, his headache would go away.

There came a time when he woke to the knowledge he was getting better. The girl was holding a bowl of steaming, sweet-smelling water under his nose. She dipped her fingers in the bowl and brushed them against his forehead. He remembered someone holding his head under a towel. The smell hovered between nice and nasty. Friar's Balsam, the name came back with the steam from the bowl. Was it a plant? Might it grow here in the mountains?

"Balsam?" he asked before repeating the word with an initial V for the Greek sound.

The girl turned her attention from his forehead to his eyes. Her eyes smiled at him. Then she placed the bowl on the earth floor by the bed and picked up a piece of slate and a chip of stone. Carefully she scratched the letters of a word. She held up the slate for Alex to read and then pointed at herself.

"Roxanne? You?" he asked before enunciating his own name clearly. He'd guessed she was deaf but she might be able to lip-read. "Alex," he repeated with exaggerated movements of his mouth.

She cast her eyes upwards, closed them under raised eyebrows and uttered a sharp tut sound, made by clicking her tongue against the roof of her mouth. Her mouth was wide; her top lip overhung the full bottom lip. It covered two slightly protruding top teeth. There was something irresistibly appealing about the way - he stopped himself from continuing the thought. He pulled himself together sharply. She was offering him the slate and the chip of stone. With his left hand, he wrote his name as best he could. "Alexander," he said, showing her the slate. "Alex."

Her mouth began a slow journey into a broad smile. He felt a urgent desire to cover her smile with his mouth. But she was a child! Apart from that, what was he doing? His mind scrabbled back to the reality of the moment. He was on a mission. He had to find Lenny and the *andartes*. He struggled to a sitting position, feeling stabs of pain. His head swam.

"Goddammit." The word could not contain the full force of his frustration but his expression certainly had an effect on Roxanne. She was ordering him back into bed, with fierce arm movements while uttering guttural sounds which didn't sound like Greek. Was it perhaps Albanian? Or Turkish? He knew the history of Northern Epirus. A mixed population under the Ottoman yoke which had come to an end only 30 years ago. More likely, he now suspected, she'd never learnt to speak; she could have been born profoundly deaf. He felt a surge of sympathy, which obliterated for a moment any thought of his own predicament. With his eyes and hands, he tried to convey many things. He understood her; he was grateful for her nursing; he knew he had to rest to recover; he'd be a good patient and lie back in bed. Roxanne was smiling at his efforts to communicate. By the time he was lying back in bed, with Roxanne sponging his forehead with cold water, Alex felt they understood each other on a level that didn't need words or signs. He felt safe with her in a way that reminded him of his early childhood, before he was sent away to school; he'd lived in a kind of cave in those years, sheltered from the harsh realities of the world. There were dangers in this feeling of safety; he should stay on his guard. Not just his training but his experience of life had taught him never to become dependent on anyone but himself. But it was hard to stay awake. Objects swam in and out of his vision. The cave entrance was fringed by black ivy, shapes picked out by moonlight, sometimes shining like metal in sunlight. He was alone; then he wasn't. He was awake; then he wasn't. Roxanne came and went.

After a while, he stayed awake for longer. When it was daylight, he set himself the task of studying his surroundings, the habitual routine of an SOE operative. He made a mental inventory of the cave's meagre furnishings: the two frayed rag mats on the beaten earth floor; the wooden pegs hammered into crevices in the rock walls, on which hung – and he listed the objects: a battered straw hat, a rubberised cape, his own battledress jacket, a coil of rope, two skirts or maybe dresses, one navy, one brown, a faded pair of grey trousers, a rusty lantern. On the floor stood a single pair of large gumboots. The sight of these tugged at Alex's attention. A man around? There were two beds in the cave, and he was lying on one of them. If the owner of the boots returned, how would he respond? Alex shelved the thought. Live in the moment, he told himself. He was adept at this.

Beyond Roxanne's bed and nearer the entrance was the 'kitchen', a bench where Roxanne warmed milk on a small gas ring. A blue-painted, semi-circular and lidded tin was fixed to the wall over a basin. It had a small brass tap above its bottom rim. Roxanne filled the tin with water from a pitcher. He had no idea where she found the water to do this. In a row on a small shelf, there were a few rusty-looking tins of different shapes. He identified, through close observation over time, the contents of three of them: sugar, rice, and coffee. Opposite the kitchen lay what Alex thought of as the bathroom area. There was a cane-seated chair beside a rickety wooden table on which stood an enamel bowl, a tall ewer and a carved wooden stand holding a cracked mirror. It was here that Roxanne prepared to wash his face and hands, and deal with his bandages. It was here, too, she looked after, in a sketchy way, her own face, hands and hair. Alex liked to watch her movements. She pulled a brush vigorously through her thick brown curls, before twisting the locks into a wide plait which she fastened in place with long pins, high at the back of her head. Her fingers were always scrabbling after the stray curls that fell behind her ears and either side of the knob of bone at the top of her spine, but she never succeeded in getting these wayward locks to stay within the plait. All was then gathered up and hidden from sight by her plain, brown scarf. The movements happened so quickly that Alex was never certain how exactly she tied the scarf. It lay low and tight on her forehead with the two ends somehow crossed, brought forward over her chin, then back again into a knot. He much preferred the sight of Roxanne early in the morning, or at the end of the day, without the scarf covering her head and hiding so much of her face. Without the scarf he thought of her as a young girl; wearing the scarf, she became a woman. Both Roxannes were gentle and cheerful nurses.

She did not appear to be worried by his presence, or his feverish state. Yet what did she know of him? Did she have any contact with the resistance? It seemed unlikely. Apart from the goats, the two of them appeared to be alone, out of sight and mind of anyone for many miles around. As he drifted in and out of sleep, Alex found that his initial anxiety about making contact with Lenny as soon as possible was fading. There was nothing he could do until he was fit enough to leave the cave and Roxanne's care. For the time being, all was well.

He followed Roxanne's comings and goings carefully. He learnt her routine: up early and out, presumably to do whatever was necessary with the goats, then back to help him hobble along the shelf, around a protrusion in the rock wall, to a rocky dell shielded by bushes to relieve himself. Even if Roxanne hadn't waited just out of sight, he wouldn't have felt the slightest stir of embarrassment. Unlike the careful measures he took with Joan to maintain bathroom privacy, he was at ease with Roxanne. It was just the two of them, living high on the rock walls of a gorge, part of nature, sharing an eyrie.

Alex was in no hurry to get better, re-start his war. He liked the way he'd dropped off the map, out of history. For the moment, he had everything he needed. Breakfast was a bowl of bread in warm milk and a tiny cup of black coffee, he sitting up in bed, she on a stool. He liked watching her going about her various tasks, keeping the cave clean and tidy. She brought armfuls of plants into the cave which she tied in bundles and hung from a rod wedged at an angle in a corner. These were the source of the infusions she concocted, first grinding the herbs in a wooden pestle and mortar, then adding them to the water she'd boiled in a small, long-handled, tin beaker on the gas ring.

Sometimes the scene mingled with memories of childhood. Roxanne, tilting his chin with two fingers while holding a glass of some herbal concoction to his lips, became Nurse Watson. *You poor little mite.* He heard two grown-ups in consultation. He couldn't attend a funeral because he was in quarantine. He heard the word and understood its meaning and ever afterwards the sound meant itchy spots and a gaping hole in the pit of his stomach. His mother had left him behind. She hadn't warned him. She'd been ill and died without his knowing. Now he couldn't reach her ever again. The best thing to do was not to let his mind go in her direction. He'd maintained this discipline throughout childhood. It was only now, bedbound in the cave, faint echoes of his loss haunted the edge of his awareness. He needed to stir himself into action.

"No," he said firmly to Roxanne when she wanted to help him back to bed after a visit to the rocky dell. He sat down on the bench outside the cave. "Here. Fine."

She raised her eyebrows, twisted her mouth and shrugged in a comical way; it was as though she wanted to amuse him. She pointed at the sky and made whirling movements with her arms. German planes? he asked, by hunching his shoulders and ducking. No, that wasn't it. She stooped and limped in a circle. He guessed she was conveying something like *you may think you're fit but ...* He clenched his fist and made the muscles of his free arm bulge. She gave a short, derisory laugh. He acted as though he would stand up and fight but staggered on his weak ankle. She tossed her head and gave a triumphant smile. Seizing the woven shoulder bag which she always carried on her day's errands, she strode away from the cave, raising a hand without turning as she rounded the shoulder of rock that bounded the cave to the north. How small she looked, she who loomed so large in his present life.

The quiet of the gorge returned. Sitting outside, he registered the difference in the quality of the quiet to the silence of the cave. It held the faintest hint of life other than himself. A distant pattering of stones and the sound of bells signalled the whereabouts of the goats, the throaty croak of a raven passing close overhead made him feel he was part of the natural scene. He closed his eyes for a moment. Were it not for the strength of the sun and the grandeur of the landscape, he might be in the Brecon Beacons where he'd spent time training. The thought made him consider his position with fresh concentration. How long had he been in Roxanne's care? He had no idea. He must stop being so lethargic. After all, he'd got himself away from the point where he'd fallen; he could surely get himself to Glikopigi. Today he'd make the attempt.

First, he needed to prepare. He must take water and food. What about his pack? Had he jumped with a pack? Had he a gun? He had a knife, he was sure. He'd cut the ropes of the 'chute. Sitting on the bench, he looked down to check what he was wearing, feeling as though he'd been absent from his body, though not its pain, for a long time. His boots were on his feet, dusty, scuffed, unlaced. He was wearing trousers, summer kit; a sleeveless vest; no shirt. He knew his jacket was hung up on a hook inside the cave. His stick, the stout branch of hazel, was resting against the bench beside him. He used it to get to his feet but a feeling of hot sickness swept over him and his vision clouded. A moment of recovery was necessary. *And he'd thought he was fit enough to walk away from here*! He chided himself for his ill-founded optimism. He needed another day's rest. When his nausea had passed, he limped back into the cave. His bed greeted him like an old friend. *Home again*. Perhaps he could see out the rest of the war living here with Roxanne! The thought made him smile wryly at himself. He knew there was a part of him that would relish the life of a hermit, one with a she-hermit alongside.

He lay in bed, on the edge of sleep. He wasn't sure if the heaviness he felt came from his own heightened temperature or from the atmosphere. The oblong of light at the cave's entrance held none of its usual clarity. Something bad may have happened to his vision that turned daylight to dusk. It was only when he heard the first faint roll of thunder that he realised a storm was brewing. The next time he was fully awake, the storm was overhead. Tremendous rolls of thunders reverberated all around; flashes of light illuminated the greyness at the mouth of the cave. Alex imagined the eye of the storm moving up and down the gorge and around the peaks of the surrounding mountains, its thunder roaring deep inside their limestone hearts, shaking cisterns full of snowmelt, making scree scatter and rocks fall. He imagined the collapse of the cave's roof; he would be immured within, never to be found. But Roxanne ... where was she? Out in the storm. People get struck by lightning. It happens. Alex saw her on a high mountain path, a narrow ledge. He saw the lightning flicker down, making its unerring path straight onto the head of the small girl. He watched the figure, like a puppet, fall down, down, down ... With a supreme effort, he pulled his mind away from the sight. Roxanne would be alright. Storms in the mountains were common. She was used to them, surely.

As the thunder moved further away, the rain began. He could see sheets of rain at the mouth of the cave. Soothed by the sound of rushing water, he was slipping into a deep sleep, when he was aware that Roxanne had appeared at the mouth of the cave. She was silhouetted against the twilight, pulling off her headscarf. She was clearly wet through; her clothes were moulded to her body. He watched as she unpinned her hair and squeezed water from the plait. She unlaced her bodice, peeled off her blouse and stepped out of her skirt. She kicked off the shoes she was wearing that day. She usually went barefoot. Had she sensed a storm was coming? He recalled her miming of the morning and now understood her message. She'd forecast not German planes but thunder. The shoes joined the heap of clothes in the water gathering on the ledge and lapping at the entrance to the cave. She grasped herself around her chest – for warmth, it seemed, rather than modesty. Modesty didn't come into it, he came to realise. Delicately she tiptoed into the cave, across both rag mats, not towards her own plank bed but towards his. She climbed in and lay down beside him as though it were the most natural thing in the world. Her teeth were chattering. She was making sounds of what he could only identify as desire. She made it clear, in the way she turned her body and pulled his good arm around her, that he was to curl up behind her and keep her warm. At the time, there seemed to be no alternative but to follow her lead. They slept.

I CHAPTER THREE

Alex emerged from a damp sleep to find himself alone. He lay for a moment collecting his thoughts, gathering them in, piling them carefully one top of the other as though building a cairn to mark a route over a mountain. To be alone in bed shouldn't surprise him. He was on active service. In northern Greece. Whatever had happened to him – yes, a mis-timed, mis-placed landing - was simply a temporary setback. Any moment he would be on track again, with a clear head. Perhaps he had been sick – yes, and he'd hurt himself. But he was getting better. He was alone, yes, but only for the moment. There was someone around who was helping him: a nice person, young, female. His feeling of abandonment must come from the memories he'd been having of his mother – or rather, of her absence. He'd dreamt vividly, too. Joan had been present. They'd made love. Certainly they had made love.

Now he was fully awake and the light at the cave entrance showed it was well into the morning. Roxanne – the name of his present nurse came with a little burst of pleasure to the forefront of his mind - cheerful little Roxanne would be bringing him coffee any minute. He would surprise her by being up and outside on the bench, waiting for her. Feeling well enough for the effort, he struggled into a sitting position on the side of the bed. The sling for his arm lay on the floor by his boots. He gazed unseeingly at the sling, while he registered a small, round mark on the sheet to the left of his thigh. He became aware not only of the penny-sized, rust-coloured stain lodged between a blue and a white stripe but the uncomfortable feeling of stickiness in his groin. A fleeting vision came to mind. He remembered small brown feet stepping across the rag mat towards his bed. Surely she had not climbed into his bed? He turned his mind swiftly back to Joan to avoid whatever it was that hovered at the edge of consciousness.

Joan, poor Joan. He'd left her on her own. An abandoned bride. He'd had no choice in the matter, of course; *don't you know there's a war on*, and all that. But once again he chided himself for not getting the intended letter written to her in Cairo. He knew she'd be watching out every day for the bicycle whirling down the hill to the farm; the click of the latch on the garden gate; the postman reaching into his satchel as he came to the door. Was he called Bill? Was he the son of the Pinhoe butcher? Slightly simple, so not required for active service. On his last short leave, Alex had begun to get to know a few of the locals. Salt of the earth, his stepmother would call them, although she'd never stoop to invite them into the farmhouse.

A series of unusual sounds brought Alex up short. Dogs barking, hooves clattering on stones, hoarse shouts. After a moment, a dark figure – a short, stocky man – stood in the entrance to the cave. Alex struggled to his feet, feeling defenceless. The man stopped short, evidently shocked to see him. There was a second's silence as though the cave itself was waiting for an explanation. Then the man bent his head and stormed into the cave, letting loose a string of staccato words as Roxanne, panting, appeared behind him. She darted around the man to stand in front of Alex, her arms spread wide, uttering sounds from deep within her throat. The man was in a whirl of anger, throwing whatever came into his hands to the right and left; clothes from the hooks, sheets from the beds, towels, Alex's sling, his battledress jacket, his stick. The rod wedged across a corner of the cave's roof was the next to go. The rod was hurled out of the cave, scattering bunches of herbs in its wake.

Alex put a hand on Roxanne's shoulder to show her that he was not worried by this dervish of a man. He guessed he was her father and the usual occupier of 'his' bed. If he could summon enough Greek, he would bring calm to the scene, something he was known to be good at. What were the words he needed? *Please don't worry about your daughter's safety. She has sheltered me. No-one has seen me here. She's a wonderful girl, an excellent nurse, I'm most grateful and I shall leave at once. Can you help me get away?*

Alex waited patiently for a chance to intervene, his hand still resting on Roxanne's shoulder. She turned and looked up at him. Her eyes seemed to be shouting messages which he tried to interpret. Then she turned away. While her father continued ranting, she stuffed the sheets and towels from the floor into a large bag which she dumped outside. *Laundry,* thought Alex. She brought a full bag into the cave and began unloading tins. *Shopping.* This, he understood, was how this cave life worked. It was an outpost, distant from the village but dependent on it. It was similar to the shepherding life in the region of France he was familiar with. With a renewed sense of urgency, he focused on the chance Roxanne's father presented. The word for horse came to him and he tried it out. "*Alogo?*" He repeated it several times at increasing volume until he was heard.

The man gazed up at Alex, the tin beaker he was about to throw out of the cave poised in his hand. "*Alogo? Nein! Moolari!*" His face cleared. The change in his demeanour was startling. "Telis," he said, patting his chest. There followed a stream of words and signs. Roxanne joined in, but not in a helpful way. It seemed that she was arguing with her father who was pushing her away while urging Alex outside where he had to step over all the things that had been hurled out in anger. A pitifully thin, grey mule was tethered loosely to the bench.

A few moments later, Alex had been helped onto the mule, the laundry was strapped to the saddle behind him, and Telis was leading the mule along the ledge towards the shoulder of rock where the path to the village began. Just before they rounded the corner, Alex twisted to look back. He hoped to see Roxanne waving goodbye. But no; she was sitting hunched on the bench, her head in her hands. He vowed he would return to thank her, once he'd established his position with the *andartes.*

It was exhilarating to be out in the open air and moving. The atmosphere was clear. Every rock and crevice on the opposite wall of the gorge was so sharply defined it felt as though you could reach over and touch it. The serrated skyline was darkly crisp against a resounding blue. What a treat to be here. At such moments one could be grateful to the war. In fact, he always was grateful to the war. He'd be bored out of his mind by ordinary life. He felt a surge of excitement at the prospect of finding Lenny and the *andartes.* This wouldn't be difficult, if he went about it carefully. Well before they reached Glikopigi, he'd chat - chat? *Communicate* in some way with Telis and learn what help he could provide.

Alex was a good rider, he'd nearly joined a cavalry regiment, following in his grandfather's footsteps. But he had never ridden a mule on a path that barely existed, on the precipitous wall of a deep gorge. Moreover, he was sitting side-saddle, not on leather but on a structure made of padded wooden battens, rigidly uncomfortable. Every so often Telis slapped the mule's haunches, uttering some urgent command. Alex didn't think it at all a good idea to hurry the animal. He favoured the slow and careful way the mule picked a path across scree, around pinnacles of rock and through the gullies which the night's rain had drilled down the mountainside. If he ever glanced to his left, the steepness of the descent to the gorge floor turned his stomach.

An hour or so after leaving the cave, the path took them in a slow curve around the mountain to leave the gorge behind. The landscape opened up, a vista of distant heights and lower, wooded slopes. Telis pointed away to the north. *Deutsch,* he said, and shook his fist. Then he pointed to the east, in the direction they were heading around the flank of the mountain. *Glikopigi,* he said with emphasis, *good, good.* Alex could not at first see a village. Then he made out a collection of faint, grey shapes lodged in a crease on the mountainside, like rocks caught in the act of falling. *Glikopigi,* repeated Telis, before embarking on what sounded like the exposition of a plan. Alex registered a few words but it wasn't until they were within a kilometre or so of the village that he fully understood. Telis led the mule off the path and up through a copse – rowan? Cherry? - to a small, half-ruined stone hut hidden among elderberry bushes and tangles of bramble and old man's beard. This, it became clear, was the mule's stable. This was where Alex would stay until someone called Ileana was found. From the signs Telis made and the words Alex could pick out, it seemed that Roxanne and Ileana were sisters but they were not Telis's daughters. Roxanne – as Alex knew – could not hear or talk. Ileana – oh, Ileana could speak English *farsi*. When he'd first learnt the expression, Alex had been enchanted with its ancient derivation. *She speaks like a Pharisee*. That would certainly make his life easier. He understood that Telis, the mule and the bundle of laundry were going on to the village. Alex would find a place to lie down at the back of the stable. With that, he was helped down from the mule, handed his jacket and stick, had his back slapped – it was more like a shove in the direction of the hut – and Telis had gone.

He listened to the sounds of the mule's departure as the familiar quiet flowed back in. He was alone again in this majestic landscape, safe but on the edge of danger. Germans to the north, Lenny and the *andartes* to the south. And friends or foes in the village?

I CHAPTER FOUR

Exploring his new surroundings, Alex found something that filled him with joy: water. To the side of the stable, several short planks of wood tacked onto a frame covered a deep stone well. Hanging on the stable's wall was a bucket with a length of frayed rope tied around its handle. Built against the wall was a stone trough. He even found a sliver of green soap on the edge of the trough. Soon he was giving himself the first strip wash he'd had since leaving Cairo.

Not content with scrubbing away at his matted hair, a week's growth of beard, his filthy limbs and sweaty body, he also threw his vest, pants and socks into the trough. Later, they would dry in no time when draped on the surrounding bushes. With the help of his stick, he trod them – like grapes, he thought, remembering France - in time to the music he could hear in his head. What was it? A hymn. *Lord of all hopefulness, Lord of all Joy, be there in our hearts, Lord, at the break of the day.* That was it. He was back in the school chapel, singing lustily. His voice had broken early and he'd relished the way he could express his growing strength through singing. *Basso profundo in a few years*, prophesised Baccy Breath, geography stroke choir master.

Whose hands were so skilled at the plane and the lathe... Your bliss in our hearts, Lord ...

He wasn't getting all the words but he certainly had the tune. He was full of hope and, to his surprise, very little pain. His ankle was taking his weight. Better still, his shoulder, without the sling, was giving him only the faintest twinge every now and again. This was a remarkable improvement since – since *the break of the day*.

"No, you have it wrong."

He heard the voice clearly. It was not in his head. It was not Telis. It was a female voice, speaking English. It came from somewhere behind him. He laid his hand on the stable wall to steady himself.

"The plane and the lathe are in the second verse."

He didn't dare turn; he was all too aware of the sight he presented. It was a female voice. And now it was singing.

"Lord of all hopefulness, Lord of all joy
Whose trust, ever childlike, no cares could destroy
Be there at our waking, and give us, we pray,
Your bliss in our hearts, Lord, at the break of the day."

Sweetly throaty, mezzo soprano. Knowing the hymn? Ileana might be fluent in English, but to know the words of an English hymn was most unlikely.

"Please do not be disturbed. I have brought clothes for you. I leave them here. I will return." The voice added, in a smiling kind of singsong, *"At the eve of the day."*

He heard a rustle and then the soft thud of something being dropped on the ground behind him.

"But I have my uniform." But by the time he'd found his own voice to utter these words, he was alone again.

The questions crowding to be answered had to wait until sunset when the owner of the voice approached once again through the bushes. She was carrying a basket and telling him, in her disarmingly lilting and accented speech, what she'd brought. Ileana, now he was facing her, turned out to be a tall, black-haired beauty. Besides his awareness that she'd seen him naked, it was her appearance which left him struggling for words. He felt like an open-mouthed village idiot as he followed her to the lean-to at the back of the stable where earlier he'd found a plank bed like the ones in the cave, a couple of wooden chairs and a table. While she talked brightly, he helped her carry the chairs and the table to the flat ground in front of the stable. She set the table with two glasses, a carafe of wine, a hunk of bread and a plate of white cheese. Then she sat down. Her smile emphasised the generosity of her wide mouth, and the regularity of her small, white teeth. She swept a long-fingered hand gracefully, palm uppermost, over the table like a conjuror revealing a banquet from a tiny box.

Alex remained standing, his hands on the back rail of his chair. He called up a vision of Roxanne's little figure, her rough, square hands. How could Ileana be her sister?

"Is something wrong?" she asked, her eyebrows twisting towards her hairline.

Her thick, dark, glossy hair was like a tamed version of Roxanne's; it lay neatly coiled at the nape of her neck.

"I do not poison you!" Her eyes laughed at him.

"Oh, I didn't imagine ..."

"Won't you sit?"

Alex sat.

She regarded him, waiting for him to speak.

"You," he began before he'd decided quite how to proceed. *You are the most beautiful woman I've ever encountered. What are you doing here, in this rough outback of the war?*

After a pause that was probably shorter than he imagined, he managed to speak. "You're not English. The hymn?" She would think him moronic.

"I will explain," she replied.

Over the next hour, as the sun set behind the receding, blue-grey lines of mountain ridges, Ileana explained. First, she talked of the English governess who'd taught her in Bucharest, a Miss Scantlebury, the daughter of a clergyman from North Devon. "Manners, deportment, Dickens, Trollope, folk songs and hymns. This is why I like to speak English." No members of the Romanian family ever called her by her Christian name, although they knew what it was: Charlotte, pronounced with a sh. On Miss Scantlebury's birthday each year, a special pudding was made, which shared her first name. "Apple with toasted breadcrumbs on the top. Simply delicious."

Breadcrumbs. I'm in a country occupied by the Germans, in a mountain hideout, hearing about *puddings.* His bemusement must have shown on his face for Ileana went on, "Yes, I know it is strange. Roxanne and I were born and brought up in Bucharest. Our father is the elder brother of Aristotle. Aristotelis in Greek, Telis for short."

"Ah." Alex had a sudden vision of Telis. That he should be called after the Ancient Greek philosopher was as incongruous as the fact that Roxanne and Ileana were sisters.

"Our father had business in Bucharest, and he married a Romanian, our mother, in 1919 when life was beginning to return to normal."

Ileana talked of her grandfather, an *emboros* who imported and exported wool, olive oil, hemp, many, many things. She waved grandly towards the horizon. "Here, there, everywhere," she said. "Not long ago, we were all in the Ottoman Empire, Greeks, Vlachs, Turks, Serbs. Our father carried on the business. He was a clever man and profited in the war. He spoke Turkish, German and Italian, as well as Romanian and Greek. He made sure that I was brought up speaking many languages, too. For my parents, the saddest thing was Roxanne."

Roxanne had been deaf from birth, as he'd suspected, and had never learnt to talk properly. "I can understand her, though," said Ileana. "And when our parents were taken away ..." She stopped, her expression guarded.

Alex tried to work out what had happened when and where; interwar politics in the Balkans had been part of his briefing, but right at this moment, with the last rays of the sun shining through the glass carafe of wine and Ileana sitting disturbingly close, their knees almost touching under the table, he could not bring anything to mind beyond his concern for a family tragedy, whatever form it had taken.

"In Bucharest in the 30s," she began but faltered. "They were very difficult times. The government kept changing. First one side, then another. People went to prison, were deported. Disappeared. My father was involved with the wrong people. That is to say, the right people at the wrong time."

Alex raised both hands, indicating she didn't have to tell him more.

"I have not spoken like this for so long. The people here, they all have their own troubles, especially now with this war, first the Italians, now the Germans. It is good for me to speak English." But she lapsed into silence, her eyes on the horizon.

Alex was never usually at a loss but here with Ileana, with the wine, the sunset, the immense landscape, and the hints of a different and more difficult history than his own, he could only sit and wait for her to continue.

"We should be talking about you, how I can help. Do you need a doctor? People knew of the aeroplane. There were different rumours. We heard that something went wrong. Supplies went missing. They thought you'd fallen down a sink hole."

Alex felt a chill which must have shown on his face. Ileana went on, "Yes. A sink hole. There are two on the mountain. Straight down, one, two thousand feet. Like a chimney. Sheep fall down them."

The chill prickled his body as he imagined what might have happened to him.

"There is no escape from a sink hole. You were lucky. According to Telis, who understood this from Roxanne, you landed in what we call the Big Ravine and she got you to the cave. You must have been with her over a week!"

"She was very kind. She nursed me."

"Nursed you?"

"Yes. She made up special herbal potions for me."

Ileana looked worried by this. She explained that Roxanne wanted to become known as the best herbalist in the area, dispensing the most effective remedies. Her obsession suited their uncle Telis. He found it useful that she was keen to stay in the cave, keeping an eye on the goats in the summer months, while it gave her the opportunity to gather the rare plants that grew in the gorge. But, sadly, Roxanne had no great understanding of plants and was overbold in her trials.

Alex recalled one particular concoction that had the colour of tea and the smell of decomposing spinach. *Drink up*, signed Roxanne. Could this be why he'd passed the days in such a muddled haze and, in marked contrast, felt so well today, having missed his morning's herbal drink?

Ileana's eyes were on him. "I am afraid Roxanne is a little, how shall I put it, simple?"

Alex felt suddenly sad for Roxanne. He remembered how she had tried to prevent Telis taking him away. Locked in her silent world, living removed from the village, she'd valued his company. There was nothing malevolent about her wish to try out her remedies on him. The drugged sleep they induced may even have helped him heal.

"She was kind to me," he said. "Her intentions were good."

"Yes," said Ileana. "The road to hell?"

"Paved with them, I know." Alex poured more wine into their glasses. How extraordinary it was to be sitting here at this sunset hour, relishing a drink with such an alluring companion. They could be in a pre-war Paris pavement café. The thought brought him up short. He was not in a pre-war pavement café. He was a soldier on a mission. He should be with Lenny on the other side of the mountain. He remembered Telis's rage at finding him in the cave. "If you in the village thought I'd fallen down a sink hole, Telis must have been stunned to see me alive."

"Yes, he was angry and alarmed. Roxanne should have come straight back to the village as soon as she found you, instead of sheltering you. Her reputation for one thing. We have a strict code of conduct here and we women have to be very careful indeed to guard our virtue and our good name. Roxanne has no understanding of this. But apart from that, more *important* than that, the *andartes* needed to know at once that you were alive and needed help. Now more than a week has gone past since the drop."

The immediate plan was for the local leader of the resistance fighters to meet Alex. "His name is Kapetan Philipas – Captain Philip," Ileana told him. "He's a rough man. He acts and speaks like a wolf but you can trust him. He will come tomorrow and take you to wherever you have to be."

And would the two of them meet again? The look they exchanged held this despairing, wartime question. Then Ileana left and Alex was alone, his mind full of the look and sound of her, her eyes and mouth telling her story, while he made himself recall his Cairo briefing. He had to get himself back on duty.

I CHAPTER FIVE

Alex had determined to go over in his mind all the information he had been given in Cairo, and before that in London, in preparation for this mission. But he only managed to summon up the chap in the Baker Street room with boarded-up windows. Major Blewitt kept repeating 'a spot of bother' in Alex's memory, alternating with insistent visions of the two daughters of Telis. He fell asleep on the plank bed – even more uncomfortable than the one in the cave – and entertained a series of complicated dreams where he lay beside, under, and sometimes on top of a girl who wasn't quite Joan, nor Roxanne, nor Ileana. She had something of all three, an intoxicating mixture.

When Ileana appeared in the open doorway of the lean-to, the rising sun making a halo of her hair, he was aware of a shameful rush of blood to his face. It was as though she'd witnessed his night's dreams.

"I have woken you?"

He mumbled a reply.

"Kapetan Philipas wants me to bring you to the village. He will meet you at our house. You are to wear these clothes, not your uniform." She laid a pair of brown trousers and an olive-green shirt at the foot of his bed. "I will wait outside."

She sounded stilted, as though she wanted to distance herself from him.

"Thank you," he said, in Greek.

Ileana smiled briefly in recognition of the effort and turned swiftly. Her skirt swirled about her knees as she left the room.

When he was ready, he found her waiting a short distance from the front of the stable, tactfully watching the sunrise. He splashed water on his face from the bucket she'd filled for him from the well. The icy temperature made him shudder. "That's the coldest water I've ever encountered," he said.

"It comes from deep. At home we arrange hot water for you."

Did she think he smelt? He hoped the sharp smell of naphthalene coming from the clothes he was wearing overcame bodily odours.

"You need a belt. Telis will find one."

She led the way along the narrow path. They walked in silence. This worried Alex. She had been so chatty the previous evening. Had she decided he wasn't worth the effort of remembering her English? He wanted to say something that would ease them back into conversation but his dreamworld had catapulted them into a closeness that didn't match the reality. He could hardly ask her if her breasts were as pertly shaped as the ones he'd cupped in the night.

He concentrated on placing his stick on firm ground at each step. The path wound its way through copses of hazel and rowan trees and across grassy glades where butterflies flittered among sage and thyme bushes. Roxanne had given him sage tea, one of her more pleasant concoctions.

After about fifteen minutes of gentle walking, Ileana stopped, holding up her hand in warning.

"We'll be out of the trees in a moment. I have left a sack here for you to carry."

His expression must have made his questions obvious for she went on to explain. From a distance he must look like a villager. There were some people in Glikopigi who must not know that the British soldier was alive and being sheltered by Telis's family.

Sheltered by Telis's family? Alex's spirits lifted, then fell. He'd be close to Ileana. On the other hand, he had a job to do. "But what about the group? I must join them. My radio operator. He'll be with them in Tesserahori."

Ileana closed her eyes, titled her chin. "*Ela, paidhaki mou,*" she said. Come, my little child. Alex followed her meekly, carrying a bulging but not heavy sack. His disguise.

"Keep your head low. Do not stop, do not look around. We'll be within the walls of our house very soon."

Alex saw what Ileana meant when they arrived at Telis's house, the first in the village coming from the direction of the gorge. Set into high stone walls, a double wooden door under a stone-slab roof, a sort of lych-gate, opened onto a paved courtyard where runner beans and onions grew in raised beds set against the large, square, house.

"Safe now," she breathed, bolting the courtyard door behind them. "No-one can see us. But shush until we are inside."

The house, built of stone the colour of the mountainside, stood squarely in front of them. Sun-blistered, once green, shutters were half-closed on the four windows of the top storey and completely shut on the ground floor, one either side of the porticoed front door. This gave the house a frowning, forbidding look. Not welcoming, Alex thought. More like a prison? Ileana took the sack from him and led him around the house to a further building, small and single-storied. Smoke rose from a tall chimney set on one side of its stone-slab roof. A woman in black appeared at the open door. She uttered a wail, drawing it out from a high note to fade away in what Alex guessed was a mixture of greeting, interrogation, admonishment and invitation. He and Ileana were ushered inside and told to sit at a table covered in a bright, red and yellow, patterned oil cloth. The woman – small, hunched, dressed in black, with a Hansel and Gretel witch's nose – bustled about the room, chattering excitedly. Something was cooking in a black, cast-iron pot hanging over the wood fire burning in a whitewashed alcove. A hot meal! He desperately hoped he'd be given a bowl of whatever the pot contained, a big bowl to be served at once. He savoured the smell – onions? tomatoes? – as he listened intently to the words flying back and forth, trying to pick out something he might understand. Every so often Ileana shot explanations in his direction. *Great-aunt. Bean soup. Difficult times. Hens. Eggs. Philipas here soon. No cheese. All gone to Germans in camp.*

"Camp? What camp, where?" asked Alex, getting in the question fast but the flow of Greek had passed on.

Philipas angry. Naughty girl, Roxanne. Ileana, good, clever. Ileana's eyes smiled at him.

He had a plate of bean soup in front of him when he learnt the location of the camp. Great-aunt was standing in front of the fire with her. Ileana was sitting opposite him. Only Alex had a bowl of soup.

"Aren't you having any?" said Alex at the same time as Ileana spoke.

"The nearest Germans are at Stavrogoni," said Ileana, but she'd also heard Alex's last question and added, "No. That's not our way."

"Meaning crossroads?" He wanted to demonstrate he did understand some Greek when spoken slowly. "Tell your aunt it's delicious."

"It's on the road to Ioannina."

"Will you eat later?"

"Not exactly crossroads. More cross-corner."

"Cross-talk more like," said Alex, aiming to make Ileana smile at the overlap in their quick exchange. He felt they had developed a special kind of understanding, which had nothing to do with spoken language.

The sound of heavy hammering came from the direction of the lych-gate. Ileana sprang to her feet and left the room. To his dismay, Great-aunt whipped away Alex's unfinished bowl of soup. She then obliterated all other signs of food. The cast-iron pot was put behind a curtain in the corner of the room. Then she went to stand in front of the fire in the alcove with her hands folded one on top of the other, palms uppermost, just below the waistline of her bibbed, black apron; a statue of domestic obedience.

Alex scrambled to his feet as Kapetan Philipas entered, followed by Ileana. Automatically, Alex stood to attention, aware that he was wearing someone else's floppy trousers and a strangely patterned shirt. For a brief half-second he was examined by ice-blue eyes before Philipas took two strides into the room, clasped Alex by his upper arms, and pushed him back into his chair.

Philipas dragged a chair from the table, whirled it around and sat down on it with his crossed arms resting on the chair's back rail. The creaking of the chair was the only sound. The room itself seemed to be waiting for Philipas to speak. Alex didn't want to be seen scrutinising the general – no, not a general, he was a self-styled captain but he felt to Alex like a top-ranking, commanding officer of great power. It wasn't just the size of the man, well over six foot and wide with it. The power came from the glare of his narrowed eyes. Thick black eyebrows grew together above his bulbous nose. His hairline was low on his forehead. In fact, his face was almost completely hidden in a surrounding thicket of wild, grizzled hair – beard and moustache completed the circle. Alex watched his lips, edged with spittle, moving within their hairy framework. Philipas had launched himself into an excited diatribe. Alex felt transfixed, a mouse mesmerised by a buzzard. This wasn't an unknown feeling. He'd met bullies all his life and had perfected his technique of dealing with them. He would not let himself be intimidated by this much larger, much older man. After all, the British army in the shape of Alex had come to aid the Greek resistance.

He eased himself to sit more comfortably at the table, giving himself room to cross his legs. "I am afraid, Kapetan, you will have to excuse me. I have only a little classical Greek. I will need to learn." He looked across at Ileana with a smile. Bring in the women; they always have a civilising influence.

The Kapetan responded by barking an order and Great-aunt and Ileana made for the door. Alex got to his feet and intervened. He ushered Ileana to the table. "We are lucky to have Ileana to translate for us," he said to Philipas.

While Great-aunt left the room, Ileana stood at the table looking unhappy. He'd put her in a difficult position. Women should not be part of a discussion of important matters, particularly in this setting. Yet without her, how did Philipas expect the two of them to understand each other? It had become a battle of wills. Alex knew that subtle little shifts in position can make big differences to a situation. Alex drew back a chair for Ileana to sit down. She glanced at the captain. He nodded. She sat down. The atmosphere in the room settled.

Alex detailed the kind of help he required from Philipas, and relished the way Ileana's mobile face expressed her translations.

"I need a mule and a guide to help me up and over the mountain."

"I need to meet up with my radio operator."

"I need an up-to-date map of the area."

"I need to know the details of your last operation. Was it successful? Any casualties? What expertise is there in the group?"

"Are you short of supplies? Give me details of specific requirements and I can get them signalled to London, once I meet up with my radio operator."

Ileana kept up well, and Alex felt satisfied save for the way everything he said seemed unworthy of an answer.

Philipas eventually broke his silence. He leant forward, folded his arms on the table and spoke slowly and clearly, pausing for Ileana to translate every few words.

"My dear mister ... imbecile of a royalist ... oh, sorry!" said Ileana, "I shouldn't have ..." But now she had to catch up. "You do not understand ...the smallest gram ... of our situation. You must ... stay here ... lock and key ...not go ... nowhere, I mean, anywhere. The scoundrels, vagabonds? What should I say? The *very bad* men ...Tessarahori ... will be made ... to handover ... the gold ... the guns ... the shoes .... they stole. The thieving bastards."

Only when he had been locked in a cellar beneath the main house did he understand his own situation, down to the smallest part of it. He'd become Philipas's prisoner, a pawn in the deadly battle between different wings of the resistance, a battle which had been fully explained to him in Cairo where he'd been far too hot to follow complex details. He'd ended up with a left-wing band, led by communists. Lenny was with the monarchists on the other side of the mountain. In Philipas's eyes, Alex was a monarchist, an enemy in a more pertinent way than any German. Britain was led by a king and Alex was British.

What irony! Alex thought back to his undergraduate days in Oxford before the war. He'd thought of himself as a communist, having joined a group which studied the 1848 communist manifesto of Marx and Engels in the light of 20th century history to date. Some members of the group, in particular an excitable economist called Brodie, argued for the complete demolition of capitalism by means of all-out revolution (off with their heads) which would happen – by the sound of it – on Tuesday week. A bloke called Wilkinson was an advocate of gradual change from the bottom of society up. Wilkinson often quoted Rosa Luxemburg's speech of 1918. Alex stayed silent in the meetings. He liked the approach of Jesus of Nazareth better than anything he'd come across since school chapel days. The non-violent actions of Mahatma Gandhi appealed to him, too; the Salt March of 1930 had made a deep impression. In spite of these influences, he'd left university to become a soldier. "Where's the courage of your convictions?" asked Wilkinson. Alex winced.

Wilkinson, at the outbreak of war, became a Conscientious Objector. "War cannot be ended by war, nor situations improved by it," he told Alex when they met in a London pub in 1939. He was obviously quoting someone else.

Now Alex the soldier, the killer of men, had let himself become a prisoner. It could be argued that it wasn't his fault that he'd landed in a ravine that led to a gorge which led to Roxanne in her cave and to Ileana in Telis's house and Kapetan Philipas. There was no element of choice along the way. Yet there was a pattern to it - one that he would contemplate later.

He looked around the cellar. He was sharing it with wide shelves laden with dried and drying vegetables: pulses, onions, who knows what. There was a high window, too high to look out of unless he could climb on something. He could only sit on a lower shelf, hunched under the one above and look out through a curtain of drying stalks and leaves. The door was locked and barred on the outside. He was most certainly a prisoner. Did he mind? No. He was under the same roof as Ileana and she was letting herself into the cellar at this very moment.

"Don't worry. I have a key too!"

I   CHAPTER SIX

Greece, 1943. Alex wrote slowly and neatly, school-boy style.

My dearest darling Joan

I have no idea when or <u>if</u> you will read this letter but I'm writing it all the same. At the moment, the likelihood of getting anything through to the outside world is nil. I'm a prisoner! But not at the hands of the Germans. Unfortunately, I've got in with a splinter group of resistance fighters who are at loggerheads with the group I should be with. Something of a hornet's nest. This is not like it was in France where I could get messages to you easily enough by wireless. Here, at this moment, that's not possible. However, I do feel safe. It seems far from the war, though there is a terrible absence of food. People are rake-thin, starving, poverty-stricken, lots of black-clad widows. Children go barefoot.

Alex had a momentary image of Roxanne's small brown feet. Ileana's feet, narrow and bony, no longer filled the pre-war shoes which she wore on Sundays. Bought in Bucharest, she told him, just before she had to leave.

There's a young woman about your age called Illy Anna (no idea how she spells her name) who has let me have this paper from a school exercise book. A story there I'll relate later. First, I must tell you what's brought me to this sorry pass.

Alex stopped writing for a moment. A letter home should be short, non-communicative. No wounds, no illness, no bad luck. No young women. But then – he wasn't really writing to Joan with any expectation she would ever get to read it. It was pure self-indulgence. It brought her close to him, and took him back to his last leave with her. Best of all, thinking what to write passed the oceans of time spent alone.

It's amazing to think we were together not that long ago.

Was it a month? Six weeks? He'd lost count. The few days in Telis's cellar seemed like a month ago now. But it was probably only week since he'd been moved to this room above the kitchen. After re-reading what he'd written, he crossed out *what's brought me to this sorry pass*. In its place he wrote *how much I love you*.

His pencil had a small plug of rubber eraser at one end which he didn't bother to use. This was a first draft. He would eventually write the whole thing in pen and ink, if Ileana could find such things. He played with the pencil, balancing it between the fingers of his right hand. His shoulder no longer hurt, he noticed. Sling and ankle bandage had been discarded, though he still walked with a limp. Not that there was any chance of walking further than a couple of paces across the room to peer out of a crack in the closed shutters of the window he was not allowed to open. The village must not learn of his presence here. However, he could spy on the village through the jagged split in the wood of one shutter. A jigsaw of stone-slabbed roofs and walls fell away below, giving glimpses of cobbled alleyways twisting between the houses. He could watch people coming and going about their business of survival, driving goats out onto the mountainside in the morning, bringing them back at night, leading mules laden with brushwood, bulging sacks, fodder; the men carried loads on their backs, the women on their heads; the children scampered between the houses, knocking for entry on the tall wooden doors set in courtyard walls. The walls hid the houses one from the other, drawing a clear line between communal and private lives. However, he could sometimes see evidence of a bush telegraph in action. Watching so often over time, he realised the women of two houses in his line of vision signalled to each other from their upper windows. Ileana told him that German patrols could never approach without the village getting at least forty-five minutes' warning. The members of the family in the lowest house acted as sentry, taking turns with binoculars trained on the opposite mountainside. Visitors on horseback or riding mules could be seen as distant specks, following the zigzag path down to the river and then disappearing from view as they crossed the stone-arched bridge. They appeared again at the crest of the hill just below the village.

He had many questions for Ileana when she brought food and water once a day and emptied – to his embarrassment - his slop bowl and flower-decorated chamber pot. Ileana was not as practical nor as down-to-earth as Joan – nor as Roxanne, for that matter. But her company, during the little time she could spend with him, made him feel alive. She called him Aleko, and was teaching him Greek. She could only understand his classical Greek if he wrote down what he wanted to say. His pronunciation, learnt at school and university, made her laugh. She had a way of tilting her head back and clasping her hands at these moments. He loved to provoke her laughter.

My dearest darling Joan, he re-read to bring his wayward mind back to the task in hand.

On one side of the pencil there was gold lettering down its length: VENUS DRAWING MADE IN CANADA HB. A Canadian pencil had been bought in Bucharest and was now being used by an Englishman in Greece – quite a journey. Ileana said it belonged not to her but to Roxanne. In Bucharest, Roxanne had been good at drawing. It was her way of communicating. Did she stay in the gorge all the time, Alex wanted to know. No, only in the summer months. Soon the cave would be abandoned for the winter. Roxanne and the goats would return to the village. The winter in Glikopigi was very cold. The pathways were icy. There was permanent snow on the top of the mountain. He learnt these things in snippets between her chores. Frequently, a coarse shout would be heard from the courtyard. She always obeyed the summons of Telis and Great-aunt at once. The sound of the key turning in the lock and the clank of the door's iron bar as she departed made him feel more solitary than he had before her swift visits.

When winter set in, would he still be a prisoner? No. Well before that, he would do what he had to do: turn Ileana into a prisoner in his stead, take the key and sneak away. He frequently imagined the steps necessary to execute his plan. He would get into position by the door holding the bedsheet. As she came in with the tray, he would grab her. Sheet and belt would secure her to a leg of the iron bedstead. The pillow case in her mouth would stop her screaming. He would lock her into the room and sneak away. He would surely find his way up and over the mountain to link up with Lenny.

The trouble was that each time he ran over the necessary moves, his imagination played havoc with the plan. He hugged Ileana instead of pinning her arms behind her back. He kissed her mouth rather than stuff it with the pillow case. He threw her down on the bed instead of the floor. Sometimes he didn't even do this. He saw the two of them sneaking away together, up and over the mountain. Other times, he got away by himself but became lost on the mountain, or fell down a sink hole. Imagining this last fate all too clearly, he turned his mind back to the letter and Joan.

How lucky I am that I met you!

He crossed out *lucky* and substituted *glad.* Sink-holes were forgotten as he remembered their first meeting. It was the kind of unlikely crossing of paths that happen in wartime: he an Oxford graduate, soldier and saboteur, just back from blowing up factories in France; she, the only child of Devon farmers still living at home but at that moment staying with a cousin in Wimbledon. They came across each other in a nightclub, pressed by the crowd into the same corner. Joan stepped backwards onto Alex's foot and lost her balance. "Sorry!" she exclaimed. He quickly steadied her, holding her around her waist. He felt a fold of soft flesh before he let go. It was he who should have apologised. Her weight on his foot had caused him to shout a word he would never normally use in female company. She went on saying 'Sorry!' when they danced together on the central dancefloor, as well as at their subsequent meetings and on honeymoon. In all other ways, Joan was supremely self-confident but the difference between them in size – she was slightly taller as well as heavier - remained all wrong as far as she was concerned. Alex foresaw a lifetime of convincing her that she was just what he desired.

You are what I always wanted.

He remembered the desert of his teenage years. At school, the only females were in the kitchen, strictly out of bounds. The holidays were spent with his father, his new wife Amanda, and their two children born soon after their marriage. They lived at the end of a mile-long track in the Brecon Beacons. His father, gassed in the war and shell-shocked, sat alone in a darkened room, skinning and stuffing birds and small mammals. Amanda, who'd been a Red Cross nurse – they'd met before Alex's mother had caught 'flu and died – devoted her life to her new family in which Alex was the odd one out. So he passed the long hours of his holidays in an attic room, making scenery out of plywood for his elaborate train set and constructing complex bridges, buildings, cars and pulley systems with Meccano. He did not realise the full extent of his isolation until he saw it in retrospect at Oxford. The two friends, Josef and William, who befriended him at the start, introduced him to communism and *girls*. To begin with, he was equally fascinated by both. Girls liked him instantly, without his having to do anything more arduous than look into their eyes and listen. The only snag was the girls that Josef and William knew became boring company after the first few occasions; these were the town girls. Their talk was free-flowing and inconsequential. In contrast, the few girls attending courses in higher education at Oxford were heavy-going; they stared intently at him, pressing him for views on subjects on which he held no views at all. Even though they weren't allowed to be college members, these young women were sharper and more earnest than the undergraduates he knew. It was easier to follow the lead of an American fellow classicist, who gave him the address of a place in an Oxford suburb where transactions were simple and he learnt a lot.

You are what I always dreamt of.

Joan was wonderfully straightforward in love-making. When he'd said something appreciative to this effect, she replied with a laugh, "What else do you expect of someone who was brought up on a farm?" He found her pragmatic approach to life refreshing. Yes, I'll marry you, she said, the third time they met. Alex was momentarily taken aback; he didn't think he'd actually asked – well, not in so many words, but never mind, it was a good idea. People were marrying, left, right and centre, as though there'd be no tomorrow. A quick, registry office marriage was what Joan wanted, and so it happened; arranged and carried out just a month before he flew to Cairo. They'd spent a total of three nights together; their first, in the Strand Palace hotel (an air raid warning wailed half way through their love-making, fortunately a false alarm) followed by two nights the following weekend when he joined Joan in Devon.

Sitting on the side of his iron bed, he relived his last leave. He remembered his excitement and impatience during the train journey from Waterloo to Exeter. One of the FANYs in the office booked him a third-class seat on the 3.30 pm train. Even so, he had to argue the toss with the fellow he found occupying his reserved sea at Waterloo. He was much the same age as Alex but he was obviously not a serviceman on leave. His slicked-down hair and a widely-striped suit gave his enterprise away. The bag he retrieved from the luggage rack was probably stuffed with silk stockings and other black market goodies. Alex didn't feel bad at turfing the spiv out to join the sailors crammed with their kit bags the length of the carriage.

The journey had taken hours, stopping and starting constantly between stations. It was nearly dark when the train drew in to Exeter St David's. He had another long wait in a long queue for the Pinhoe bus. When the bus came at last and he managed to get a seat, it was after ten. A glimmer of light still hung in the sky above the Haldon Hills. Ahead, the hooded headlamps cast narrow beams down the dark and empty streets and, without any warning, a powerful sadness flooded every inch of his body.

He had the same feeling now, with far more cause. Back then, he'd let the thought of parting spoil the happiness of the present. What a tragic waste! But the sadness hadn't lasted. Walking up the hill towards Colebrook Farm, he'd recaptured his excitement. The night air held the smell of newmown hay. As he unlatched the garden gate, he felt like a boy about to open a present. Joan must have been watching from the hall window for she appeared at the front door. Somewhere in the middle of the garden path they met in each other's arms.

I CHAPTER SEVEN

Ileana was at the door, pink-cheeked with the importance of her message. "Kapetan Philpas ! He wants to speak with you!"

Alex sprang to his feet. He'd been hoping to see the captain for days. He'd only seen him once since arriving at Telis's house and that had been an unsatisfactory meeting. All his questions had been brushed aside. "Wait, wait," Philipas repeated, using English for emphasis. Ileana had shrugged her shoulders. She wasn't able to supply any answers.

Following Ileana down the outside staircase, he ran over his much-rehearsed demands. It might be wildly optimistic but he hoped he could turn the situation in his favour. He needed Philipas to help him link up with Lenny and the other group or groups, so he could organise a united operation against the Germans, as Cairo had ordered.

Kapetan Philipas was, as on the previous occasion, sitting astride a chair, his arms crossed on the back rail. He looked as though he was not at home with furniture.

"Good afternoon," said Alex, giving the captain his wide, pleasant smile.

Philipas said something in response, followed by a barked command in English. "Siddown."

Alex sat.

"Kawfee?" he asked.

It turned out that Philipas had worked on the Canadian Pacific Railway. This didn't mean he had much English. He depended on Ileana for translation. While Great-aunt brewed up coffee, the three-cornered conversation began. Philipas apologised for the conditions he'd been forced to keep Alex in. The reasons for such inhospitable treatment were many. There were known informers in the village who, if they got wind of the presence of a British soldier in their midst, would take pleasure in handing him over to the Germans. Apart from these rats, cuckolds, bastards (Ileana translated the list carefully), there was the group which had taken possession of Lennie and the supplies. The list of epithets was repeated.

What he, Kapetan Philipas, must do now was to keep Alex safely under lock and key until he had secured the safe return of the supplies that had been stolen.

So that was it. The supplies, as well as politics, were the cause of the rivalry between groups.

"And Lenny?" put in Alex quickly before Philipas had taken breath. "My wireless operator? I need to report back to London. He could be brought here?"

Philipas brooded on this. Great-aunt brought the coffee, muttering something which Ileana translated. "She says sorry for the taste. It's ground from acorns as well as coffee beans. Coffee's like gold," she added.

"Gold!" repeated Philipas, picking up the word. "How much gold?"

"I can do nothing without Lenny," said Alex, seeing an opening.

Philipas spoke some more and Ileana translated. "He wants to know the value of the gold. How many sovereigns were dropped?"

"I have no idea. They are all sealed in containers. I've never thought to ask. It's not my remit."

"It is good to give him a figure. Otherwise, he will not co-operate. He will leave Lenny with EDES and the monarchists. He will use your – how do we say? - expertliness – exclusively for EAM and the communists. You cannot do anything without the help of the Kapetan."

Philipas beamed. "She right. You see?"

Alex hazarded a figure. "Roughly, five hundred," he said, hoping his guess would be persuasive. "And of course, with Lenny here, I can contact London for a further drop."

That did the trick. The atmosphere in the room lightened and Great-aunt was ordered to bring wine and glasses.

After this meeting, Alex was allowed more freedom, but only within the confines of the courtyard walls. He could sit under the vine outside the kitchen and watch Ileana as she hung up sheets to dry. He learnt that she did the washing for a number of households. This entailed carrying large bundles down to the *vrisi*, the spring by a row of stone troughs in the lower part of the village. "For my keep," she explained. Telis was a childless widow. He'd taken in Ileana and Roxanne after their parents disappeared. Through compassion, said Ileana; for his own benefit, thought Alex. The sight of Ileana's reddened knuckles after a morning spent at the *vrisi*, made him wish her delicate hands could be spared. Roxanne would make a better washerwoman. He suggested this.

"And I in the gorge with the goats?" Ileana raised her dark eyebrows at the thought. "Better here. Besides, I am engaged to be married. When peace comes, I'll be gone."

Engaged! He had no right to feel as though he'd been socked in the guts. Who was this man who had the rights of ownership over Ileana? "Gone? Where?" was all he felt able to ask.

"To Tessarahori."

She went on to explain. Although Nikos came from the other side of the mountain, he'd joined Philipas's band of *andartes*.

"So he's a communist?"

"He's not committed, politically. He simply wants to fight the Germans in whatever way he can. He joined the Glikopigi group of ELAS to be near me."

Alex retired to his room above the washhouse to take this in. He had no right to feel devastated, but he couldn't help it.

My dearest, darling Joan, he re-read. But he failed to get back to writing the letter. *Wretched, bloody war.* It had taken him away from his wife and given him a glimpse of something now doubly forbidden.

I CHAPTER EIGHT

For the next few days, Alex stayed in his room, even though Ileana tried to persuade him to keep her company. She didn't understand why he would no longer sit in the shady courtyard corner by the washhouse, or help him pin the washing on the lines strung across the courtyard.

"But I like to talk eengleesh with you," she told him. Sometimes he thought she was exaggerating her accent to charm him. He was content to be charmed.

"I'm writing a letter to my wife." There was no need to emphasise the fact he was married. Ileana had known from the start. The reminder was directed at himself.

But the letter didn't progress. If he turned his mind to Joan, Ileana got in the way. If he thought of Ileana, Joan intervened. He'd somehow lost all sense of purpose. In his struggle to remember the reason why he was here at all, he went over in his mind the days in Cairo. The way the first two attempts had been aborted had taken on a new significance. He ran the scenes as he remembered them as though through a film projector.

Geared up and looking like a pair of Michelin men, he and Lenny sat side by side in the belly of the Liberator. Hugging their knees, they braced their feet against metal ribs in the floor. In front of them the bomb bay was open in readiness for the drop. They peered down, hoping to catch a glimpse of the bonfires which would signal this was the right place. The pilot made a low pass. Moonlight picked out rocky slopes holding a wide, bowl-shaped valley. A disc of silver water flashed past under the fuselage. Apart from this, all was darkness below. The plane climbed again.

The day before, the failure had been due to lack of visibility. The mountains had been shrouded in thick cloud. This time the absence of signals was the problem. Either their navigation was faulty and they had not located the dropping ground, or it was being staked out by the Germans, somehow alerted to the mission. Both were equally possible.

The pilot took the plane in low for another pass over the plateau. There were no signalling lights. The pilot climbed and turned south. Lenny looked up, his ginger eyebrows raised in question. Alex shook his head. The opening was closed, the crew returned to their positions, and Alex and Lenny unbuckled their parachute packs. They stretched out as near to the horizontal as they could among the canisters. Lenny folded his arms across his chest and was asleep in minutes. Alex pulled his imaginary cape over his head and shoulders, the trick learnt in childhood for dispelling the knot of tension in his chest.

Back at the Canal aerodrome, everything had to be unloaded into a shed: the canisters of equipment and supplies, the wireless set, the parachutes and their rucksacks. "It has to be third time lucky," Alex said as they struggled out of their flight gear.

"Sure thing," said Lenny. He sounded confident, or at least unworried. Nothing seemed to upset the New Zealander, not even the sunburn he'd suffered in just a few days of Egyptian sun. The skin was peeling off his nose. Even his hair glowed a fiercer orange, as though it had been sunburnt too.

Jeeps were waiting to take them and the crew back to the city. Lenny and the pilot took the first jeep; the crew, the second; Alex, on his own, the third. He had to go straight to HQ before going to his own billet for the sleep he was longing for. They'd meet up in the evening at the bar they'd been taken to on their arrival from England. It was full of people coming and going from all stations in the Middle East, and no-one would be surprised to see them back so soon. Aborted missions were commonplace as was the oft-repeated quotation: *We also serve who only stand and wait.*

Although it was still not yet ten o'clock, the heat was overpowering. It was made worse by the strong south wind: a full-on sirocco, going about its usual business of making everyone bad-tempered. Fine, red sand from the desert stung the face, got up the nostrils and clogged the lungs. As they neared the narrow streets of the city centre, the driver was constantly brought to a halt by knots of violently arguing men. At one point a cluster of wildly gesticulating Arabs turned on the vehicle instead of each other. They banged on the bonnet and shouted what were clearly the rudest of obscenities, judging by their gestures.

While waiting to see the officer on duty, Alex sat in the shaded courtyard of the old colonial building that housed the Middle East command, He lit a cigarette.

Cigarettes! He hadn't thought about them since landing in Greece. He recalled the pleasure of smoking. The business of tapping the cigarette out of the pack, the flick of the lighter, the first, deep inbreath of nicotine. He used to smoke as many as he wanted knowing that he could replenish his supplies.

The way to give up cigarettes was to get stuck in a gorge. He must report that to Joan. He'd begun the letter in his head in Cairo; it was still not written. How was he to describe for her all that had happened, in a few, censor-proof sentences?

Supplies. That was the key to the situation with Kapetan Philipas. He needed to remember the details of the conversation he'd had while waiting to be briefed at the Cairo headquarters. A bloke had approached with his hand held out. He'd introduced himself. Willetts, like Alex, was a captain with a parachutist's badge on his uniform.

They'd sat on a bench together. Willets had seemed nervous, talking rapidly and in low tones. It had crossed Alex's name he might be a double agent. Two aborted attempts at landing – had something gone wrong on purpose? Although the courtyard was sheltered on three sides by the wings of the headquarters building, the sirocco was gusting through the wrought iron gates. Sand was eddying around their feet.

"Rotten bad luck," said Willetts.

Alex didn't reply at once. But as Willetts didn't offer anything more, Alex said, "That's how it goes, sometimes."

"Your second time, too."

Alex nodded. He drew on his cigarette and funnelled the smoke out of the corner of his mouth, away from his neighbour on the bench

"Thought I'd take the chance to expand a bit on background. Could help you."

Willetts had a concerned look on his face, like someone about to help another over a dangerous chasm. "You see, it's not quite as straightforward as you've been told."

"No?"

"Did you meet Myers?"

"The chap who oversaw the railway viaduct do? Gorgopotamo?"

"That's the bloke."

"I know he was taken out recently and has gone back to London but no, I didn't meet him."

Willetts was grinding his heel in the sand that was eddying by the bench.

"Know anything about him? Beyond the Gorgo deal, that is?"

"No." Alex had decided he was going to play safe with Willetts. Learn as much as he could from him and give nothing back.

Willetts seemed to come to some sort of inner decision. He reached in his top pocket, unbuttoned the flap, took out a small piece of paper which had been torn from a 1942 diary.

"Apologies if you've done your homework and have it all pat. But if you're anything like me, you'll find this useful to refer to – at the start, at least."

Alex glanced at the pencilled notes, recognising the list of initials. By each, there was an explanation of what they meant. The initials and explanations were written in both alphabets, the Greek and the Latin. "Thanks," he said, folding up the paper and putting it in his trouser pocket.

"The thing is, there's been a significant difference of opinion. Different viewpoints."

Willetts came to a halt. He looked carefully around the courtyard, then got to his feet to check behind the two palms either side of the bench. "Can't be too careful," he said, sitting down again.

Alex was puzzled. "I know about rivalries between the groups of *andartes*. Supplies for one group being taken by another. That's my brief. Sort them out."

"So it is, so it is. But the different viewpoints I have in mind are between the Foreign Office and My ... well, I can put it another way. Between military aims and political aims. Myers and -". He looked around in every direction before whispering the name of the prime minister in Alex's ear.

Willetts seemed too disturbed to be a double agent. He was gathering sand into small mounds with the side of his boots, before knocking the mounds flat. "Military and political," prompted Alex.

"Yes. The thing is." He stopped for a second but, when he started again, he seemed to have come to a decision about how much or little to tell. He spoke quickly, urgently, in a low voice as though as to baffle an eavesdropper. "Myers was in the field for eight months or more, he understood the situation very well, he had a good team. I was one of them. After Gorgopotamos, we blew up another part of the same line, the Salonika-Pireus line. That was a year ago. Myers was going to leave, but he was asked to stay on which he did do until just the other day. Any rate, all this is to say, Myers had a very good understanding of the situation on the ground. It was imperative to get all the different groups to act together as one united band to achieve the military objective of defeating Germany. Makes sense, doesn't it?"

Alex nodded.

"But have you any idea how difficult it is to just get two individual Greeks to agree on anything. Each man is his own master. To get two *groups* into an agreement is almost impossible. Myers was faced with at least four groups, all with different aims for the post-war government of Greece. That's still the situation. The biggest group is communist-led - check the notes in your pocket later. It's made up of ELAS, the guerrilla force in the mountains, and EAM, the political arm, the organisers in Athens. Their aim – it's become very clear in the last months – is to take over control of all groups and establish communist rule in the country after the Germans leave. At the opposite end of the spectrum are the Royalists who want the King to return. Then there are the republicans who don't want the king back on any grounds. And there are those who want a plebiscite for the nation to decide democratically if they want a monarchy or not. Myers who is just a soldier, albeit a bloody good one, found himself entangled in politics. He managed – and it took ages – to get the fighters of all political persuasions to work together. He called these National Bands. We spent weeks tramping to and fro across the mountains, eventually getting all the groups to sign something he'd concocted called the National Bands Agreement. He used supply drops like good behaviour treats. Sign on the dotted line and you'll get more ammunition, guns and gold sovereigns." He paused, looking dejected. "But it all started to fall apart almost as soon as the agreement was signed."

He stubbed out his cigarette and asked Alex for another. "Myers thinks there'll be civil war. In fact, the groups are beginning to fight each other right now. He thinks the only way Greece can be saved from itself is a clear demonstration by the British government of impartiality. All the bands of *andartes* agree on one thing: they are convinced we the British back the return of the King. They look at our monarchy as proof of our attitude. Our *official* line is that we're impartial but here," he indicated the main building with a nod, "they don't see that. They're still stuck in 1941 when the whole of Greece rallied to the support of the King and government under Metaxas. They don't realise how attitudes in the country have changed. They can't envisage a communist take-over here, or if they do, they want to bolster resistance to it. They formed the impression that Myers had misinterpreted the situation in the field, or - at worst – was a communist sympathiser."

He lapsed into silence and his feet came to rest, one polished leather shoe on top of the other. Alex thought he understood his anxiety. He was clearly a Myers man, and Myers was banished.

"Thank you," he said carefully. "But I'm not clear how this affects me."

"There were no lights, were there. That's why you didn't make the drop."

Alex removed a particle of tobacco from his tongue and flicked it away. The possible significance of the lack of lights sank in. He hadn't until now imagined that the reception committee at the landing ground might not be composed of fighters welcoming British officers and supplies with open arms. Which group had Cairo been in touch with to arrange the drop? That was a pertinent question to ask but Willetts' attention was on a soldier who'd appeared at the doorway of the main building.

"That's us," he said. They went in together.

My dearest darling Joan. The letter was still not written although, as Kapetan Philipas's prisoner, he had plenty of time. In Cairo a previous attempt had landed in the wastepaper basket. He had fully intended to finish it after the briefing. Instead he'd slept all day. On waking, he'd gone at once to meet Lenny in the hotel bar, as arranged.

47

Lenny pushed a beer towards him. "Good man." Alex grasped the chilled glass, and then lay his wet palm on his forehead. "I don't know whether to drink the stuff or chuck it over me."

Lenny agreed, with his gap-toothed smile. "Yeah, a shock to the system, this heat."

"We won't even have time to get used to it. We're up for another bash tomorrow. There's a plane free so we must grab it while the moon's right. We're scheduled for 9 p.m. to arrive there about midnight."

"Good one." Lenny had put some pink ointment on his face to soothe his sunburn. He was full of questions. "What did they say about the landing ground? Did the navigator get it right?"

"They thought so. That water shining in the middle of the plateau sounded right." He didn't go into the details he'd learnt from Willetts. It was best not to share qualms about the reliability of the resistance fighters with his wireless operator. Lenny was a no-nonsense sort of fellow, who didn't tangle with the why's and wherefore's of a situation. He just wanted to do his job when and as required, then go to sleep. He had the most amazing capacity for sleep that Alex had ever come across. He only came fully alert and focussed when his head was clamped by earphones and he was at his set, twiddling for signals and tapping out messages. However, there had been the odd occasion in France when the usual pattern was upset. This was when something or somebody had got Lenny's goat. Lenny's goat was a deeply hidden, sensitive creature who, once roused, could floor the person who had got his goat. He'd been lightweight champion in his home town of Tauranga. Alex, in the bar of the Empire Hotel, remembered how Babette's brother Henri had roused Lenny's anger. Despite frequent prohibitions, he continued to use the crate that housed the wireless set as a stand for decanting wine. The firkin slipped from Henri's grasp and emptied its entire contents, a local red wine, over the crate. Alex had found it hard to stop Lenny from beating Henri to a pulp. He then spent weeks re-establishing cordial relations in the household on which he and Lenny depended for their safety. In the Greek mountains, he would make sure Lenny's goat was not disturbed.

"Let's hope it's third time lucky," said Lenny.

"We'll drink to that." Alex clicked his fingers for one of the hovering, waiters.

Lenny put his hand over his glass. "Perhaps we should we get an early night and do something relaxing tomorrow morning? A swim? A pyramid or two followed by a siesta?"

Alex raised his eyebrows in an exaggerated way. "You mean that?" He moved his attention from Lenny to the scene in the room beyond their table. There were as many glitteringly-dressed females as there were khaki-clad men, draped and sprawling in a variety of attitudes in the deep armchairs and on the arms of the chairs, gathered in groups around low tables throughout the large room. It could have been the setting of a rowdy West End party or a modern-dress performance of an operatic drinking scene. The noise level was growing louder by the minute. A man in a white tuxedo was playing ragtime on the grand piano, half-hidden by a giant palm. Alex looked back at Lenny and saw he was in agreement. Neither of them wanted an early night.

The next day they did not meet up for a swim, nor for a taxi-ride to the nearest pyramid. They met when they were picked up at their respective lodgings by the driver who was to take them to the aerodrome, one hour before their scheduled flight.

"Don't blame me," said Lenny as Alex clambered after him into the back seat of the jeep.

Whoever's fault it was, he was not up to sorting out which one of them had done something to which blame could be attached. He had no idea what had happened the night before. All he could manage was a groan, indicative of the inferno that was thumping at his temples and churning in his gut. He tried leaning his head backwards to rest against the rim of the seat. This didn't help. He leant forwards to prop his elbows on his knees and hold his head in his hands. At this moment, the driver engaged gear and the jeep shot forward. Alex was thrown onto his knees on the floor.

Lenny let out a bark of laughter which turned into a long throaty "aargh" as the jeep bounced in and out of deep potholes in the road. Now the two of them were on their knees. They struggled back onto their seats with difficulty. Lenny looked none too good. In fact, Alex feared he was about to be copiously sick. Or was his view distorted by his own state? He felt very ill.

"What happened last night?"

"Last night?" Lenny made it sound as though Alex had asked him about something that occurred the previous century.

"Where were we?"

Lenny's brow furrowed. It took a while before he said, "Here."

"What do you mean, here?" They were driving through a market square.

"Not *here*. Here. Egypt. Cairo." Lenny sank back, the effort of speech too much.

Cairo! The word brought sudden order to Alex's mind. He'd been woken and hauled out of bed to get into this jeep with Lenny. They were being driven to the airport where a plane would fly them to Greece. He felt his stomach lurch. How could he have been such a dolt as to drink too much before this mission? He was older than Lenny. Nearly twenty-six, for god's sake! A responsible officer! What had happened? Where had they been? What had they done?

Like fog slowly lifting, glimpses of people and places gradually revealed themselves alongside snippets of conversation. There was a girl called Flick.

"Actually my name is Felicity." Her dark hair was brushed in a high curling wave from her forehead, and she smelt of gardenias. She was sitting on his lap because the taxi, despite having two rows of seating behind the driver, was full. "We're pilots," said the fellow the far side of Flick. It was all coming back. The four pilots had been in Canada for training – a Pole, a Scot and two Irishmen. "Sounds like the beginning of a shaggy dog story," said the Scot as they introduced themselves. The taxi was taking them from the Empire Hotel to the apartment they shared in a suburb of Cairo called Heliopolis. "Sun city," said Alex but no-one paid any notice. Lenny also had a girl on his lap and they spent the journey locked mouth to mouth, disengaging just long enough to enter the apartment block. The pilots' flat on the top floor was large and cool, with many rooms and a huge modern refrigerator stocked with champagne. Three more girls appeared. "B.O.A.C," said the Pole in explanation of the luxury. "We've been seconded." They were flying the Armstrong Whitworth Argosy on routes from Cairo to India. "We call it the Curry Run."

"Bombay," breathed Flick in his ear. "Come with us, why don't you."

Alex felt as though he was being shown the view from the open door of a cell. One step would take him from grey imprisonment into sunlight. He was on the brink of liberation – from duty, from danger, from deprivation. Here were people of his own age having fun in the company of happy-go-lucky girls.

"As if I could," he told Flick, pulling the corners of his mouth into a rueful expression.

"You poor lamb," she said with a smile and smoothed his mouth with her generous lips. But instead of walking into the imaginary sunlit scene, he was about to board the plane which would take him to occupied Greece where he would be marooned in the northern mountains for an unknown length of time. The only means of contact with the outside world would be Lenny and his wireless.

"Right," said Lenny. "This is it." They were turning into the aerodrome.

I CHAPTER NINE

Pounding heart, bursting lungs, painful ankle – Alex was suffering. Every so often he raised his head from the rough path to catch a glimpse of the last in the line of six men disappearing through the scrub and low-growing trees. They were making their way - almost vertically, it seemed – from the back of Telis's house straight up the mountain. The pace the men set was beyond him, he was so out of condition. They would wait for him at the first spring where others would join them. Philipas hoped to muster a 20 man force.

Now that he had been accepted as a member of Philipas's band of fighters, he was back in uniform. He kept having to hitch up his trousers. The leather strap of the rifle slung on his shoulder cut into his collar bone and aggravated the remnants of pain from his botched landing weeks earlier. A cheery, young lad called Yiannis offered to carry the rifle for him. But Alex refused; he wouldn't lose face. He'd summon strength and energy from somewhere. He'd always found the first half-hour of a climb the most arduous; it put the most strain on heart and lungs. Soon he'd get back into it.

Yet he'd never gain the fitness of these men! They moved like mountain goats, even those who'd been town-dwellers. In the past week he'd got to know them. There was Byron, Vironas in Greek. Alex liked the incongruity of the name. He was a broad-shouldered butcher from Ioannina. His head seemed to be set on his shoulders without the intervening convenience of a neck. He wore a leather belt from which hung three knives of different lengths, each buckled into its own sheaf. His particular buddy was Lefteris, a long-legged man whose face in profile looked as though it been ironed flat. He and the butcher made a pair, reminding Alex of Jack Spratt and his wife. Odysseus, tall and distinguished-looking, was a retired dentist from Athens. Thanos was local. He was the village schoolmaster and the father of Yiannis. Alex found both father and son easy to get along with. He could practise his Greek with them. Then there was Nikos, Ileana's intended. It was hard to understand what she saw in him. His forehead was puckered in what looked like a permanent frown.

"Eh, Aleko!" The cry went up as he approached the spring, the first halt. Some joking remarks were made about the time he'd taken. He acknowledged the banter with a smile and a wave of his hand before thrusting his head under the water trickling from a pipe set in an upright concrete slab. The water fell into a long trough where wasps were dive-bombing the men who had perched on its edge. Someone offered him a section of an apple and made room for him.

The apple-giver was Thanos, He talked slowly and clearly, keen to help. Had Aleko found the climb difficult? How was his ankle?

"So-so," said Alex. "Hot. Tired." He failed to find the words to expand on this. His understanding had progressed more quickly than his ability to speak.

Thanos slapped his thigh. "Never mind! Soon you'll be a palikari like my Yiannis."

Palikari – Alex had heard the word several times. He understood its meaning, without exactly translating it. Wanting to prolong his lesson, he asked Thanos what time it was. Several people joined in. It was eight-thirty, ten to nine, twenty past seven. No-one wore a watch. Everyone judged the time by the distance the setting sun was from the horizon and everyone's judgment differed. The discussion turned to the hike ahead and the time it would take to reach the plateau and its lake. That's where they would rest before the long slog across the mountain to Tessarahori. They must arrive at a point before the descent to the first of the four villages well before dawn.

Alex knew the plan Philipas had outlined. It had been discussed between them, with Odysseas, Byron and Lefteris adding their views while Ileana translated. The group were to wait at an agreed look-out point while Alex and Nikos went on down to the first village. Nikos knew where to find Lenny. According to Philipas, Alex and Nikos would bring Lenny up to the look-out point before walking back across the mountain to Glikopigi, leaving Philipas and the others to capture the stolen supplies. This was not what Alex had in mind. His main aim was to persuade the two groups into peaceful collaboration.

As they continued the climb, the chance of collaboration seemed remote. The members of even this one small group were in constant argument. How they had the breath to talk at all, let alone argue, amazed Alex. The more he got to know the members of the Glikopigi group, the more he foresaw difficulties. Odysseas, in particular, was quietly disruptive. This wasn't just because he could speak English fluently. Like any dentist that Alex had ever come across, he was used to speaking without being answered. Even without a dentist's instruments in his mouth, Alex found it hard to counter Odysseas's opinions.

The next time they rested, they were on a ridge with the plateau in sight below them. Odysseas came to sit beside Alex. By now it was dark. Without a moon, the stars shone more brightly than Alex had ever seen before. If he could just detach himself from his present preoccupations, he'd be lifted into the sky to become just another pinprick of light in the universe. But Odysseas kept him firmly attached to the earth. He was presenting Alex with an alternative plan to the one Philipas proposed. Instead of returning to the look-out point with Lenny, Alex should stay concealed in Ano Kipseli, the first of the four villages. He and Lenny should wait until the raiding party had secured the cache of weapons. The element of surprise would save much bloodshed. Lenny could then establish immediate contact with London and order another drop. "Both groups will undertake to share equally. This is the only sensible course," said Odysseas. "It is not to our advantage to make enemies in Tessarahori. We need them, as often as they need us. I am a true communist. Once the Germans leave, we will establish a soviet in these mountains. Everyone will have an equal opportunity in life." He elaborated on the future he imagined.

"But Philipas," Alex kept inserting these opening words into Odysseas's steady flow whenever there was a chance. "But Philipas said ...the plan ..."

"Philipas is a military man," said Odysseas, when he eventually heard Alex. "He is not a thinker. Not a politician. In normal times, he is a postman in Ioannina."

An incongruous picture came to mind: Alex saw the captain trudging around the streets with a sackful of letters, like a black-haired and possibly malevolent Father Christmas.

Philipas was at that moment on his feet, urging everyone forward. They must reach the point above the villages before sunrise. Alex wondered if he should alert him to the confusion that Odysseas might cause but the only person who could translate for him was Odysseas himself. In any case, it was best to leave it to Philipas to discover and sort out, if need be.

As they left the lake behind, a couple of dogs barked from a further ridge which sheltered a few stone huts with conical thatched roofs. "Sarakatsani," Thanos told him. Alex understood. He knew about the shepherds who brought their sheep up to the plateau from the coastal plains for the summer months. Thanos was explaining their way of life in more detail, but Alex struggled to follow. He managed to ask, in a simple way, if any of the shepherds were members of the resistance. In the starlight Alex saw Thanos raise his chin and heard the click of his tongue; a definite no. This confirmed what he'd read and learnt from his briefing. The Greek-speaking Sarakatsani, kept themselves to themselves, following their traditional shepherding life in northern Greece, Turkey, Bulgarian, Romania. This reminded him of his first thought on learning that Ileana and her sister were from Romania. Before he learnt their history, he'd wondered if they were from a Sarakatsan family.

Although it was impossible to make out the lie of the land in any detail, Alex guessed they were passing the head of the ravine, the scene of his landing. Roughly five hundred yards to his right the ground was creased into a shallow V, a dark line against an indeterminate starlit background, possibly a glimpse of the opposite side of the gorge the ravine led into. On the return walk, he would look more carefully. It would be daylight – and he'd be with Lenny. The thought added energy to his step. He was no longer aware of any pain in his ankle. Either the rigorous exercise had helped or the new aches in his leg muscles claimed more attention. He was easily keeping pace with the man in front of him. Sometimes this was Thanos, sometimes Nikos – whoever it was, Alex had faith in their ability to choose the safest footholds over slopes of scree, across hummocky ground and boggy hollows.. There was no clear path, as far as Alex could see. Every so often they passed a cairn of stones, which must mark the way.

When they eventually reached the pass they'd been aiming for, a thin line of lemon-coloured light had appeared on the eastern horizon, making the stars fade. From here, the land descended steeply. A zigzag path over loose shale led to the ruined walls of a chapel. This was the look-out point. Rifles clattered on stone as the men settled themselves down, found places to sit and rest their backs, took off boots, unscrewed the tops of flasks, drank deeply. Philipas went around the group, giving orders.

He allowed Alex and Nikos a short rest and then ordered them to head on down for the village. After an hour of silent. fast, descent, they reached the first few houses of Ano Kipseli, the highest village in Tesserahori. Nikos went up steps to the door of the nearest house and knocked. A man in a white nightshirt appeared and let them in. His name was Panos. Lenny was asleep in a back room and Alex went on to wake him, leaving Nikos with night-shirted Panos in the kitchen.

Lenny shot awake as soon as Alex opened the door. He sat up and stared at him in utter astonishment.

"Aren't you dead?" he asked. They both laughed at this and punched each other in the chest. Lenny kept exclaiming at the sight of Alex, and asking more and more questions about what had happened. He'd spent the last few weeks in ignorance and confusion. There was not a single person able and willing to speak enough English to tell him what was going on. He'd established contact with Cairo but they were as much in the dark as he was himself. "I think they sent the Missing, Presumed Dead message to your wife."

Alex was dismayed at the thought of Joan receiving such a telegram. The sooner Lenny sent news of his safety, the better. He urged Lenny to get up and dressed.

When they joined Nikos and Panos, it was clear they'd interrupted an earnest discussion. The two men stopped talking at once. Panos bid them welcome and held a carafe of white liquid over the tiny glasses he'd set before them. It was impossible to refuse. Alex knew the drink; he'd been given *tsipouro* by Telis, and appreciated its fiery strength. Lenny said he'd been kept going by it. He raised his glass. "*Yia sas.*"

They all clinked glasses.

"Panos has given me good board and tucker but god knows what's going on here. Nikos tried to tell me, but we couldn't connect."

"Nikos? *This* Nikos?"

Alex felt disturbed by the information that Nikos had called in at Panos's house twice since Lenny had been there. His family lived in Meso Kipseli. He'd introduced Lenny to some of the local *andartes* and their leader, a Kapetan Akill something.

"Achilleas ?"

"Could be. Whatever he's called, he's all fire and brimstone and no substance," said Lenny. "He was no help in organising a search party for you. I guess he'd vanish like a puff of smoke if called on to do any sabotage. What about the lot you came over the mountain with?"

"They're about to raid the village."

"This village? Here? Why on earth?"

"To get back the supplies your group took."

Nikos was staring down at his drink. Whether he could understand the conversation or not, he seemed lost in thought.

Lenny said he hadn't realised that there was any competition between the groups. "Not my look-out," was his usual response to any strategic planning. "I just twiddle the knobs."

Alex's mind had been working fast. Philipas wouldn't launch the raid until Alex was back at the look-out point with Lenny. If Alex could get hold of Kapetan Achilleas immediately, he would persuade him to come with them to meet Philipas at the look-out point. Alex was confident that, with himself as a diplomatic intermediary and Odysseas as translator, plans for future co-operation could be put in place. Lenny would signal for supplies, in their presence, then and there. This would reassure both parties that more gold was forthcoming. All would be in accordance with their individual wishes and aims. Peaceful agreement shouldn't be difficult to achieve.

But Nikos was frowning. Did he frown all the time, or was his brow naturally furrowed? Alex still wasn't sure. Despite the frown, Nikos responded well to Alex's request. Yes, certainly he would take them to meet the captain. At this hour, Achilleas would be having a coffee in the square of Meso Kipseli. They should go at once.

The village of Meso Kipseli was almost a continuation of Ano Kipseli. They came to a square where a plane tree provided shade for a few tables and chairs outside a café. It was still early and no-one was about, not even the captain.

Nikos did not seem surprised. He urged Lenny and Alex past the tree, the café tables and chairs and into an alleyway. Fifty yards or so down the alleyway, he opened a small door set into a larger double wooden door and ushered them through. As their eyes grew used to the dark, they heard Nikos close the door behind them. The sound of a bar being slotted into place was so familiar that Alex didn't need to turn.

"Bloody hell," said Lenny, "he's locked us in!"

"He'll be back," said Alex. "Just a precautionary measure." To keep them safe from the raid? He didn't feel confident about this, though. All kinds of suspicions about Nikos were forming in his head.

Their eyes were getting used to the darkness. They were in a storeroom. Bulging sacks were stacked high against the walls. More sacks were visible on a platform that jutted out into the room, a kind of mezzanine.

Lenny was pacing about, complaining bitterly. "Why would he want to lock us in? I wasn't locked in by Panos. I could wander around the village, and was invited into homes. It was fine - or would have been if you hadn't gone missing. I didn't have the foggiest notion what I should do."

Alex had found a ladder which he rested against the edge of the platform. From the play of dim light coming in at the level, there might be a window up there. He climbed up far enough to establish that he was right.

"Hey, Lenny! "

Lenny came to the foot of the ladder. "What is it?"

"Whatever Nikos plans, we're not going to stay and find out. Give me a second."

He climbed up onto the platform and made his way, hunched under the sloping roof, to a small window at the far end.

"Come on up," he called.

The window, despite being festooned with sticky cobwebs, was easy enough to open. Its wooden frame was rotten and collapsed in Alex's hands, the glass pane shattering at his feet. They peered out. The storeroom had been built into the mountainside and there was only a drop of about eight foot to open ground. They could make their way around the back of both villages until they were within reach of Panos's house. There they might be able to rearrange a meeting with Kapetan Achilleas – without Nikos.

Once on the ground, they went into combat mode. They moved up the mountainside finding cover where they could – ruined walls, thickets of elder bushes, large boulders. A cock crowed nearby and was answered a distance away by another. Although the sun had risen, the air was still cool and fresh. Alex felt elated. He'd been out of action too long. Lenny was panting behind him, making wry comments in a hoarse whisper whenever they paused to listen for danger. That would take the form of pursuit by Nikos, although Alex had not yet had time to work out if or why Nikos had become their enemy.

They'd reached a point which Lenny thought was on a level with Panos's house when the sound of gunfire came from a point below and to the right of them. Alex had paused to listen when suddenly a fierce, cracking sound pierced his hearing and stone fragments flew off a boulder immediately in front of him. He knew at once what had happened. In his five years in the army, he had never been so close to a bullet. He felt not so much shocked as affronted.

"Bloody hell."

"Bloody fucking hell," agreed Lenny.

They ran, half-crouching, through the alleyways to Panos's house, and crashed into it. No-one was there. Alex stuffed what he could find of Lenny's belongings into his pack, and Lenny fitted the various components of the wireless into its leather case. Then they were out of the house and climbing towards the look-out point.

"Christ," said Alex, when they felt far enough up the path to pause. There had been no more gunfire.

"Was that the raid?" Lenny asked.

"It must have been the raid. Do you know where the supplies were held?"

"No. I didn't even notice how they were brought to the village from the landing place. I think there was a line of mules. I was searching for you with Panos and another bloke as long as I could."

They continued the climb in silence. Even before they reached the look-out point, they sensed that it was empty.

"Now what?" asked Lenny when this was confirmed. "Oh, look, someone's left their rifle."

"That's mine."

"And some water. Do you think they're coming back?"

"Not a clue."

"What on earth was Nikos up to? He did lock us in, didn't he?"

"Yes – but why I can't really understand. I can see he's in a difficult position. His family lives this side of the mountain but he's a member of the resistance group based in Glikopigi."

"Could he be a member of both groups?"

"From what I've been told, I think he is. But that shouldn't lead him to take a pot shot at *us*."

They were sitting at the entrance to the ruin, the sun on their faces, gazing unseeingly at the view. He could tell Lenny was not willing to delve into political details. In fact, he looked as though he would drop off to sleep at any moment.

"My only thought," Alex went on, not sure yet what he did think until he heard himself, "is that Nikos has - taken a – sort of - dislike to me."

"Ha! *Extremely* likely. Everyone does, without fail." Alex was used to being teased by Lenny.

"No, it *is* likely. Seriously. He's engaged to someone who's been translating for me."

"Oh. Ah. I begin to see."

"There's nothing in it. I mean, she and I are just good friends."

"Ah. A *She*. Just good friends."

"She's from Budapest. Greek parents. An orphan. She has a sister. They were taken in by their uncle."

"How old?"

"Middle-aged."

"No, the *girl*, idiot."

"Ileana is about 21 or 22. Roxanne – she's the one who looked after me in the gorge – she's a few years younger." Alex had a swift memory of a cloudburst, and a wet and shivering Roxanne. He hoped his face wasn't showing the sudden warmth he felt.

"I understand," said Lenny with a slow smile.

"Oh, there's nothing in it." Alex was aware he was repeating himself.

"Maybe not, as far as you're concerned. But don't think I don't know how the girls swarm in your direction. I sympathise with Nikos."

"Rot!"

"Or should I sympathise with poor Roxanne?"

"You're way off target. Anyrate, we should get going. I'm not keen to wait around, whatever Philipas and the others have been up to."

Tramping back across the mountain, Alex reflected on the past night. Had it been the spectacular failure it felt like now? Instead of getting the leaders to meet, he'd got himself sealed in a storeroom. Why had Nikos bolted the door on them? Had Philipas led a raid on the supplies? Was that what the gunfire had been about? Had there been outright warfare between the resistance fighters? A great achievement for a British liaison officer! And who had shot at them as they made their way back to the rendez-vous? He had never before felt so defeated by circumstances beyond his control.

They swung along together in single file, Alex leading the way. In daylight, it wasn't difficult to see what line to take. The earth beneath their feet had a reddish tinge which differentiated the path from the surrounding stony terrain. Cairns marked the trajectory across the high inner world of the mountain massif. The undulating ground ringed by high peaks was like a cloth held over a number of giant knees by giant fists. The map with its contours now made sense and Alex felt better. He was heading back to familiar territory – most importantly, with Lenny. They marched in step. Lenny was good company. He was no help in any decision-making process; it was his amenable acceptance of decisions that helped. It was enough for Lenny to drawl 'No worries, mate' and Alex immediately felt secure. Last night however --- a different matter. Lenny was still asking about Nikos's motives.

"I don't think you should trust that man," he said. "Jealous husbands and all that."

"They're not married!"

"Okay. All the same."

"Whatever's going on with Nikos, it has nothing to do with ---" Alex didn't want to say her name. "- anything else." He went on to expand on the local situation and the rivalry between the groups, in the country generally as well as in the local area. It was important to establish just where Nikos's loyalties lay. How he could do this was not clear to him at the moment, but he found it refreshing to talk freely in English.

"That's where I landed," he said now to Lenny, pointing westward. "At least, I think that's the start of the ravine." The slight depression in the line looped between peaks gave a glimpse through to what must be the far side of the gorge. The sun was now high enough to light up the colours of its limestone cliffs, buff and grey columns like the pipes of a cathedral's organ rising into the deeply blue sky. He had come full circle since the night he'd landed. Tonight he'd get a message through to Joan. And he'd see Ileana.

That was the successful outcome of the expedition. He and Lenny and Lenny's radio transmitter were going to be on the same side of the mountain.

I CHAPTER TEN

The expedition across the mountain altered the situation Alex found himself in. He was no longer locked in his room, although he understood he was to stay within the walls of the courtyard. There was a great deal of coming and going from the house. It was as though the *andartes* of Glikopigi had been galvanised into action by the gunfire in Tessarahori, for reasons Alex could only guess at. He was invited into the kitchen to join in discussions. Without Ileana to translate, he found it impossible to take any meaningful part. He felt like a teenager, on the fringe of important, adult decisions. He guessed his presence was tolerated as the necessary cost of receiving supplies.

During his time in France, he'd had no such misgivings about the French resistance fighters. Back in London, when briefed about his role in Greece, he'd felt full of confidence. He was the professional expert, representing the British government and army, the vital liaison that would give cohesion and purpose to a ragbag of Greek resistance fighters. In the reality of the moment, listening to the excited voices round Telis's kitchen table, he felt useless. Save for Thanos's son Yiannis, he was much younger than the other men, with no understanding of the local conditions. In fact, he had no idea at all what the *andartes* were thinking. Neither did Lenny, but the difference between them was that Lenny believed Alex knew. Alex thought it best not to reveal to Lenny the quagmire of doubt that he felt inside. From experiences in his life to date, he knew that people judged him to be fearlessly in command of a situation. He'd been called a natural leader in a report by a commanding officer at the end of his initial training.

"You could get somebody to do something they didn't want to do just by looking at them," said Lenny.

He was carrying an extra load for Alex when he said this. It was a couple of weeks after the puzzling outbreak of gunfire in the villages the other side of the mountain, and they were on their way to the *andartes'* base, a cave in the lower reaches of the gorge. Alex was overjoyed to be out, in the open, and filled with purpose. A night of heavy rain had stirred the mountainside into life. The scent of herbs – thyme, oregano – drifted on the air, which held a new chill. His spirits soared. Now he could at last concentrate on the mission. They would complete it before the month was out. The canopies of trees in the valley below showed autumn colours. It was October. The path they were following was narrow and overgrown by bushes. The easier way was along the riverbed, but that was sometimes patrolled by the Germans, at least for some of its length from the crossing to Glikopigi.

The cave when they reached it was bigger than Alex expected, and six men could lie down comfortably for the night. Equipment was stored away in a kind of sub-cave to one side. Ileana, who brought food from the village at midday, let him have the blue school exercise book and a stub of a pencil to jot down facts, figures, and make diagrams of alternative rigs of explosives on the bridge. He knew its dimensions but he had only seen a couple of fuzzy photos of the bridge, taken in 1934.

Over the next few days, life in the cave settled into a routine. Alex found it most congenial. Ileana brought food from the village and, most days after the midday meal, Alex helped her carry the tin plates down from the cave to wash them in the river. If she really didn't want his help, she could easily refuse but she seemed to like his company. They were not behaving in any way that might be considered inappropriate. Just friends, as he told Lenny. He paid no attention to the way Lenny raised his ginger eyebrows towards his thatch of ginger hair.

Washing up was not an arduous job. There were seven plates, a varying number of spoons but no knives and forks. Each of the men used his own knife if anything needed cutting. Various village women took it in turns to find something to cook for the men; usually, a kind of porridge made from cornmeal, sometimes enlivened by flecks of goat meat. Alex guessed there was competition for the job because it was funded by the British mission in the form of gold sovereigns; a pot of food cooked for the *andartes* would feed the cook's family as well.

The cave where he and Lenny were now living with the *andartes* was not the one where he'd been sheltered by Roxanne. The cave that the *andartes* used as a base lay further to the north where the gorge walls widened and the icy blue water, which rose in the springs below Telis's cave, had become a wide but shallow river which sparkled over white pebbles. Its grassy banks were overhung with plane trees. The washing-up place was on a promontory of fine shingle, a kind of riverside beach. Here, Alex could scrub the plates clean with a handful of gritty sand before Ileana washed them, with her skirt hitched up and her brown legs calf-deep in water. With Lenny, he'd once tried to bathe in the river, not imagining that water could be so bone-freezingly cold. They'd both galloped out of the water swearing at the tops of their voices. Ileana didn't seem to feel the cold, though when she sat down beside him on the bank she rubbed her toes with her long-fingered hands. He could imagine doing this for her. If he'd not been married, if the two of them had simply met here in this magical part of Greece in peacetime, then he'd better not dwell on what might have happened. Another kind of life lay out of reach, not to be contemplated.

As it was, these few occasions alone with Ileana felt like a holiday, a respite from the reason why he was there at all. All thought of war left his mind and he could forget that two hours' hike downriver lay the site of the planned sabotage: the road bridge, the key transportation link in the area. As soon as Ileana left to walk back to the village, he pulled himself back into his military role, filling his mind with the task in hand. He returned to designing the neatest, most efficient way to blow up the bridge, working from the two, over-exposed photographs taken in 1934 and produced by the Baker Street office. In the pale brown and fly-speckled photos, a man stood beside a mule in the foreground in two different attitudes, both of which, blocked the view of the central pile. This was annoying but it did not present a major difficulty. The final design would only be possible after the reconnaissance he planned to carry out at the waning of the present moon.

The equipment that would be needed was stored in what was little more than an alcove to the back and side of the cave. He'd recently blocked the entrance to the store with a large, now empty crate, a visual more than a practical deterrent to any light-fingered *andarte*. The main cave was roomy but uncomfortably crowded at night if they were all present. This didn't happen often. Apart from Lenny and himself, the others came and went, usually for a couple of nights at a time. Alex was getting to know the ones most often present. burly, blue-eyed Philipas with his shock of unruly black hair; Thanos the softly-spoken schoolmaster with his bright-eyed son Yiannis who ran everywhere at the double; Odysseas, the talkative dentist; Nikos whose eyes swivelled constantly in their sockets, ever on the alert for danger; wedge-faced Lefteris and his companion Byron, the knife-festooned butcher. When they weren't arguing excitedly in the cave, they scoured the steep hillsides with guns. Hares, pigeons and partridges added to the food the village could supply. One day Byron and Lefteris struggled back with a large, wild boar they'd shot, which made a feast. The week before Odysseas had come across a chamois caught by a log in the river at the base of a sheer cliff. It had not been dead long. This was a rare piece of luck. It was carried to the village for cooking in the communal oven and came back, over several days, in various guises – roast, stew, soup. The river's usual produce was trout. Alex imagined fishing with a rod but learnt – when he heard a loud explosion – a much easier fishing method was used. He suspected this was thanks to the powdery contents of a particular cylinder in the cave's alcove. This was when he decided to barricade the opening to the store. He could imagine the stock of explosives being rapidly diminished.

He liked to sit at the cave entrance with Ileana's exercise book. While he doodled with different combinations of explosives, he thought back to the time after his finals when he'd decided to change direction. He'd realised that he didn't have to be bound by his classics degree. He could develop his childhood interest in how things work. His father had expressed surprise when he announced he wanted to join the army as his path to engineering. "You want to kill people?" The question came as a complete surprise. As far as Alex was concerned, his father had fought in the war to end wars. The world was at peace. In the army Alex would serve king and country, travelling the world, building bridges and roads for the benefit of the empire. He did not imagine that he might one day have to kill someone. Or be killed himself.

The time he spent with Ileana made him reflect on his life in a way he never had before. Sitting with her on the riverbank they shared stories of their separate pasts. One day he told her of his shock at his father's question: *You want to kill people?* He found it easy to confide in her.

"Strange as it may sound, coming from a soldier's mouth in time of war, it had never entered my head when I joined the army that I might have to kill someone."

"No?" Ileana's eyes widened.

"No. I didn't join the army to fight anyone. I joined so that I could become an engineer."

He described how he'd always liked working out puzzles of construction. At school physics and maths had appealed to him as much as ancient history. Besides deciphering Greek and Latin and tracing the power play of gods and emperors, he'd enjoyed metalwork and carpentry. It all seemed to come down to checks and balances. How much load to put here so that, over there, will lift and the other descend.

"For me," said Ileana, "I like to watch the checks and balances between real, live people."

"Oh." The delightful way Ileana spoke sometimes got in the way of his ability to hear what she said. *Forra mee, I laeek to vaatch cheeks and um-balanzes between ree-al peeepull*s. He never tired of watching her lips shape the words. "Yes, I see what you mean," he said.

But he was conscious at the same time of an uneasy feeling. He should bring her boyfriend Nikos into the conversation. "What about Nikos? Do you have checks and balances between you?"

"Haa!" Ileana laughed. "Perhaps. But you should know that our engagement is arranged. It is not my choice. I would like to ---" She was hunting for the way to express her thought.

Alex would have liked to make suggestions. Escape? Get out of it? Run away with me?

Just then there was an explosion down river that made them both jump.

"What?"

"Fish?"

"Yes, fish."

They both realised at the same time that they had drawn very close. They needed to disentangle from the way they were holding each other's arms.

"Sorry."

"Sorry."

"I thought that was."

"So did I."

"It wasn't."

"It was fishing."

"Yes, fishing.

"Anyrate, time to."

"Yes."

"Ileana?"

"Yes."

"I love you." Had he blurted this out loud?

"I love you, too." Were those the words she'd muffled with her headscarf across her mouth?

"We musn't."

"No, we musn't."

They were standing very close to each other.

"I must go." But she didn't.

He caught her hand in his. A silent conversation lay behind their words. He could hear it in the space between them.

"I am going." She stood still, regarding him. "I wish," she began and stopped.

"So do I."

"Goodbye."

"Yes."

She turned and left without a backward glance. He felt as though he'd fallen into another ravine. He gathered up the tin plates and climbed back up to the cave.

Later, he sat with his back against the rock at the cave entrance, the exercise book open on his lap. He stared at the diagrams of different explosive rigs he'd made over the last week, but he saw instead Ileana by the river. He'd been warned of falling for local girls before he'd been dropped into France. The warning was repeated in London before he flew to Cairo. So recently married, he'd paid little attention, knowing – as he thought then – that he was in no danger. There'd be no young women among the Greek *andartes*. He'd be far from a village. If he'd put females into the picture at all, he'd imagined a lot of black-clad peasant women, bearing brushwood on their backs, as seen in a photograph enclosed in a file of background information. To find himself in the frequent company of English-speaking Ileana had been an unpremeditated challenge. She was altogether too beautiful, too graceful, too vitally present to ignore. Joan in her family's Devon farm had become almost unreachable in his thoughts, lacking all relevance. The same abrupt division had happened between school in term time and home in the holidays. Each stopped like the end of a film when he wasn't there. They still existed in theory but he packed them away as though in a box not to be opened. Instead, he listened instead to the voices in the cave behind him. He had a job to do here and he must stay alert in the present. At the same time, he could allow himself a little unseen flirtation which could harm no-one.

Inside the cave, the voices of the *andartes* were raised in intense argument, the rapid exchange of Greek sounding like machine-gun fire. He could understand some of the men better than others. That was Thanos, shouting down the others in his schoolmasterly way. The present bone of contention was not, as it often was, the class struggle and what this meant in non-industrial Greece, or who would lead the communist party once the war was over or who owned the field below the church of Ayia Paraskevi. The bone of contention today was – literally – bones: the origin of the fragments littered in the earth of the cave floor.

"That's a bloody motherfucking *goat*'s bone!" Byron sounded as though his life depended on it. "I should know."

"If that's a bloody motherfucking goat's bone, then my grandmother is a motherfucking bloody donkey!" Two blue veins stood out like knotted string on Lefteri's thin neck.

"Forgive me," said Odysseas his careful manners strained to the limit, " but that is a human tooth, and *I should know*."

The battle between butcher and dentist might have continued had not Thanos taken command. Alex found him the easiest to understand because he spoke slowly and clearly. He was expounding on the use of the cave in Paleolithic times. Alex moved to sit within the cave to listen. The earth of the cave floor, said Thanos, is full of the splinters of animal bones. Over the eons, levels have changed. The cave was once nearer the river.

"Bugger me," said Byron.

Thanos continued. Stone age men drove the wild animals of the time down from the mountain, channelling them into the gorge and trapping them at the narrow points. Any animals they managed to kill they dragged into the cave and butchered. Hence all the flints and animal bones.

Byron squinted at the flint Thanos held up for inspection. "Didn't the poor buggers have knives?"

"Po, po, po," exclaimed Lefteris. "Could you kill a man with that?"

"No, they used rocks," replied Thanos.

Alex thought of the cave's position, high above the river, sheltered by interweaving, tree-covered slopes of the mountains on either side. The *andartes* had assured him of its safety, and now that he'd heard about the prehistoric ambushes, he could understand this more clearly. No German patrol would be so foolish as to risk men venturing into the gorge, however much wider its walls were as it approached the plain. Rocks flung down from the cave to the beach where he and Ileana washed the dishes would scatter a patrol, to be picked off easily with a rifle.

Lenny was in the cave too, speaking with Yiannis. Alex liked the way Lenny and young Yiannis got on, without understanding a word of each other's language. Each day Yiannis went with Lenny up the hillside to the point where Lenny could get a signal. The boy watched intently as Lenny set up the receiver. So far there'd been only a couple of successful transmissions.

Still, the office would know all was now well and that the mission was about to be carried out. Joan would have learnt that he was alive and safe. The sudden thought of her made him feel as bad as he would have done if he'd succumbed to temptation, wrapped Ileana in his arms, let his mouth meet hers as it so longed to do and, and - and then - *nothing.* Nothing had happened. He'd been saved from a very bad mistake. As if summoned by these thoughts, Nikos, who had been absent all day, approached the cave from the direction of the village. Without a word - in fact, almost as though he hadn't seen Alex - he stumbled over his outstretched legs to the back of the cave.

Thanos greeted him. Nikos growled something in reply and sat down beside him. The two voices continued in an exchange that was brusque but amicable enough. Soon, however, their voices were raised in argument. This often happened between these two. Something or other would set it off: the way Thanos was lying at night, with his elbow in Nikos's ribs, or a daytime squabble over who'd been drinking from which tin mug. A fierce quarrel would develop swiftly. With everyone else, Thanos was mild-mannered.

Thinking about it now, with angry voices filling the cave behind him, Alex realised that Nikos was always involved. Odysseas and Yiannis remained outside any fracas, as did Philipas, and of course Lenny and Alex himself.

It might be wise to leave Nikos out of any operation on the bridge. Leaving aside his arranged engagement to Ileana, he was a disruptive individual.

I CHAPTER ELEVEN

Alex called a meeting in the cave to announce his plans for a recce to the bridge. The men he chose for his team were Philipas, Byron, Thanos and Yiannis. The Kapetan had to be included of course, although Alex thought Philipas might be more hindrance than help on an expedition that needed extreme quiet and caution, with no theatricals. Byron with his knife skills might come in useful but only if things looked like going wrong. The father and son pair, Thanos and Yiannis, were the sort of dependable and sensible chaps Alex would always want to have alongside him. Lefteris was relieved to be left out but Nikos objected strongly to being omitted. He claimed special knowledge of the bridge and the camp dating from a trial sortie carried out by another group of *andartes* based to the north-west. Thanos caught Alex's eye and raised a quizzical eyebrow.

"I regret," Alex told Nikos in his slow and careful Greek. "I prefer to keep you fresh for the big attack." He could have phrased this more gracefully but at least it bought him time. He'd think up a good reason to exclude Nikos on the night itself.

He would conduct the recce the night after next. The moon was in its last quarter. They would aim to arrive between three and four o'clock in the morning, the hours known to be the hardest for guards to maintain close watch. Vigilance drops after long and uneventful night hours and before a morning patrol takes over. Eyelids grow heavy and attention easily slips.

The hike to the bridge would take about an hour and fifty minutes, Philipas told Alex. Maybe longer, he added. Since the Germans had replaced the Italians, the path that followed the river on the stretch between the point below the cave and its entry onto the plain had not been used, either by the occupying forces or by the *andartes*. The infrequent German patrols to Glikopigi came the long way, by mule tracks from the main road, over the intervening hills, down to the river, across the old, arched bridge where the gorge widened, then up the long cobbled path and a series of steps to the village.

On the night of the recce, they found the stony path on the banks of the river hard to follow. Clouds drifted across the face of the quarter moon. In the narrow passages where cliffs plunged to meet the river bank, winter rains had washed the path entirely away, leaving shifting scree. Philipas, at the head of the single file of men, swore regularly. They would come back another way, he told Alex. "It's more difficult, but it will be safer on the Night."

Alex understood that the 'difficult way' was not so much a path as a bandit's escape route from the road, up the almost sheer northern face of the mountain to arrive at the back of Glikopigi. But more difficult than *this*? His weak ankle wobbled alarmingly on the uneven ground. Black and slippery tree roots made a deceptive lattice over the path. Fallen leaves disguised sudden, deep hollows which held pools of water from the previous night's rain. At one point Philipas bounded off, leading them up a slope of scree away from the river, to slither down the far side in a cascade of stones, landing up on the very brink of the water.

"*Seismous,*" he said in explanation.

Thanos expanded on the number of earthquakes in the region in recent years.

"But none of them serious," put in Yiannis. "Not in my lifetime at any rate."

That was 16 years or so, calculated Alex. Might it now be time for a serious earthquake? That was a useless thought. He turned his mind back to the path. This was a valuable exercise, learning how long it took between cave and bridge. *Time spent in reconnaissance is seldom wasted.* He remembered, with a wry smile, his father's precautionary words uttered at any suitable opportunity, such as driving off into unknown Welsh lanes before Alex's first term at prep school. The memory added to his feeling of impending doom.

"Good for you to get to know both ways," went on Philipas.

Alex understood the gist, even if he did not understand every word. "The Night" was the way they all referred to the planned act of sabotage. It made him think of theatricals. *It will be all right on the night.* But would it?

"Okay?" Philipas used the English word,

Alex was leaning on the stout hazel branch he'd used since his first days in the gorge with Roxanne. He straightened swiftly. "*Endaxi,*" he replied, with the best grin he could muster. *Oh God, take Thou this cup from me.* Why had this come to mind? It sprang as though from nowhere, unbidden. It summoned up an old feeling of dread, of inescapable Fate mustering its forces against him. If only he could wake up now, lying in bed next to Joan at Colebrook Farm. Devon! With its pillows of green fields and gently lowing cows!

He placed his feet more firmly on the path in Philipas' wake. The way to get out of this mood was to concentrate on the particularities of present time and place. He watched his dusty boot move forward to find the next safe footing. Grey pebbles and mossy boulders were faintly lit by the waning moon. He felt better. He reminded himself this was only a recce. They were carrying little. Each had a rifle slung over a shoulder and wore a bandolier of bullets. Alex also had a backpack in which was a tape measure the size and shape of a curling stone and Ileana's exercise book and a pencil. At the first sign of danger, they could race away up the mountain, a route so sheer no German in his right mind would follow. So promised Philipas; Alex was not convinced.

The Kapetan was surprisingly vague about the location and size of the German presence. His informant, a local goatherd, reported on the comings and goings of troops from Ioannina to the camp which lay "two cigarettes" from the road bridge. Sadly remembering his Gaulloise and Gold Flake days, Alex translated this into 15 to 20 minutes or rather less than a mile. No distance at all for vehicles. Anything going wrong, and the full force of the Germans would be upon them before they could escape. The camp was thought to house a platoon, about 50 infantrymen on average but numbers varied, depending on activities further to the north-west. The bridge was guarded night and day. An eight-man patrol was marched out from the camp, one patrol relieving the one before at eight hourly intervals. There was always one lorry and one jeep in position by the bridge, which provided a base for the men to sit and while away the hours while four men marched up and down from one end of the bridge to the other. The informant said that one patrol unit was more punctilious than the other two, and one of those two was made up of two *tembelidhes*, lazy bastards. They played cards in the lorry, drank beer, laughed and talked. But there was no knowing which unit would be on duty, either tonight or on The Night.

It was four thirty in the morning when Philipas raised his hand and brought the men to a halt. Ahead, just visible at a curve in the river Alex could see a graceful stone arch over the water. "No," said Thanos, behind him, "that's not it. That's the old way." It dated from the 18th century. He was going to add more but Philipas ordered them to stop talking. The path, now cobbled, led over the stone arch but the men continued, following a narrow goat track between the river and bushes growing in clefts of rock in the final curve of mountain. They halted before the land opened up onto the plain. Half a mile ahead they could make out the gleam of the asphalt road. Two army vehicles were parked either side of a dip in the land straight ahead and about half a mile away. This was where the river ran under the bridge. Their target.

"Okay," said Alex, now ready to take command. He'd planned this in his imagination. Philipas and Byron would stay right where they were, hidden in the lee of a bush, to cause a diversion if necessary, and provide cover. Thanos, Yiannis and Alex would creep along the river bank to the bridge, timing their approach to the moments of least attention from the guards. They watched for a while. The guards worked in pairs, starting at the furthest and opposite points on the bridge, marching in step to meet at the centre, stamping out a crisp about turn, then back to their own side. Sometimes the pattern varied. The four paused in the middle and exchanged some just audible banter. They omitted the about-turn and each pair continued to the far side of the bridge, opposite to the one where they'd started.

Alex and Thanos conferred in whispers. Whatever the pattern, it made no difference. The guards maintained a steady watch: two pairs of eyes scanned the landscape in wide sweeps, covering all points of the compass as they crossed and re-crossed the bridge.

The dangerous part of the approach was from where they now crouched to the point where Alex reckoned they'd be below the sightline of the guards fifty yards or so ahead. He chose his moment to make a dash for it, scrambling as fast as possible along the river bank, followed by Thanos and Yiannis. They stopped and straightened as soon as they considered it safe, in the lee of the bridge. They listened for a moment to the tramping of boots, then an exchange of chat. Hearing German spoken sent a sick chill through Alex.

The last time he'd been this close to the enemy had been in France. He'd been in a hay loft when a German soldier challenged the farmer who was sheltering him. The memory brought back awareness of the dangers he was courting, not just for himself but for the *andartes* who'd become his friends, and the village as a whole. Reprisals had been talked about in the cave in low voices; they hadn't wanted Alex to hear. But Alex had heard. Whole villages not far away had been burnt.

Alex remembered enough school German to understand the gist of the conversation on the bridge above. It seemed a poker game was in progress – perhaps in the lorry which showed light beneath its canvas sides. It sounded as though the guards had laid bets on the men playing. Whether he'd understood this accurately or not, Alex felt a surge of confidence. The operation was not going to be difficult. The bridge with a central pier and two cement embankments on either side was just as the photographs had led him to expect.

He waded into the river and, feeling his way carefully, found safe footing under the first span. He could not hear the men and felt entirely safe. To his relief, he could touch the underside of the first span at its midway point easily enough. He had thought he might have to use Yiannis for this, by lifting and holding the lad on his shoulders. It would not be necessary. All he had to do now was to prospect for weak points in the cement where he would place the explosive. A single span destroyed would mean the whole bridge was unusable.

He let his fingers rove over the surface of the cement above his head and soon found a jagged crack, ideal for the purpose. With his penknife, he made it deeper and longer. Chips of cement fell in the river but without any sound louder than the running of the water which, after the night's rain, swirled vigorously around the central pier. Reassuringly, and despite the sound of the water, he could hear the steady thumps of the guards' feet continuing on the bridge above him.

At his signal, Thanos and Yiannis joined him in the water to take the measurements. Yiannis held notebook and pencil and jotted down the figures. Just before they finished the job, Yiannis was overcome by a fit of sneezing and caused all three men to freeze in an agony of apprehension. The third sneeze was not followed by another; the steady thump of feet continued; Alex and Yiannis exchanged looks and immediately broke out in stifled snorts of laughter. Thanos looked stern which, with the urgent need to be silent, made their convulsions greater.

The two were still doubling over with spasms of suppressed giggles when they re-joined Philipas and Byron. Alex tried to recover the gravitas appropriate to his position but it was impossible. Somehow he'd reverted to the Alex he'd been when he was the age of Yiannis. It was wonderfully liberating.

I CHAPTER TWELVE

The morning before the night of the operation, Alex composed a message for Lenny to send Cairo: a simple coded message informing them the mission would take place at 04.00 hours local time. Yiannis wanted to go up the hill with Lenny and sit in on the transmission. He could never sit still. Alex decided he would go, too.

It was a sparkling autumn morning. Across the river, the trees and shrubs formed billows and tufts of fiery colours, a rich, Persian carpet of a hillside. Above the treeline, the lump of high land that hid the long route to the main road stood out in purplish-grey against the blue sky. Turning his gaze to the south as he climbed, Alex could see the paler, distant crags of the gorge walls. He thought he could make out a cleft on the skyline which might mark the start of the ravine down which he'd fallen; it must have been about eight weeks previously. It was hard to keep track of time, especially as he'd lost as much as two weeks through injury and befuddlement.

But now he felt a different man. If he'd been asked how he was, he'd have answered "top hole". Apart from the annoying weakness in his ankle, he was fitter than he had been for years. He could climb the steep hillside behind the cave without puffing. He felt wonderful. He was fulfilling his mission. There'd be more acts of sabotage to plan and execute. He had his team of *andartes* and seemed to be accepted by them. He knew that he had yet to work on the liaison side of things. The next step would be to organise something that would include the group from Tesserahori. That would take a more diplomatic approach than had been possible so far. But now he had a clearer idea of the mountain's geography and the people involved. His ability to communicate in Greek was far better than it had been. He would step up his lessons with Ileana.

Ileana.

Just thinking her name was enough to jolt him out of this satisfying appraisal of his situation. He was suddenly too hot; too uncomfortable; too uneasy; too impatient. He needed to see Ileana. He needed to see her today because he might not be alive tomorrow. That was the truth. No matter how sensibly and coolly he approached the night's activities, he knew it could all go wrong. He could be dead by tomorrow.

But he simply must not succumb to his feelings for Ileana. The more he tried to put her out of his mind, the more his mind returned to the image of her,

He would have to pay for falling in love with Ileana. That was the way things worked.

He told himself he was not in love with Ileana. He was married to Joan. Ileana was not to be thought about.

Yet he was thinking about her now, as he neared the place where Lenny had set up the aerial. He could see Yiannis bent over the radio transmitter, playing with the knobs as piercing whistles and crackles came and went. Alex hesitated. He could join them and enjoy the fact that at last he was sending notice of action. Or he could go on up the hillside to a promontory on which sat a small chapel. He knew Ileana sometimes lit a candle there on her way to the cave with the midday food. She said she prayed for the souls of her parents.

He would go to the chapel. It was mid-morning, probably too early for Ileana to be on her way. He could light a candle for good luck, if not with a prayer. The payment of the tinny coin in his pocket, all he carried, a tenth of a drachma, might placate the gods.

Shouts from Lenny made him hesitate. He joined them.

"You're not altering the message, are you?" Lenny asked.

"No, no, not on your Nelly!"

"Nelly?" asked Yiannis, eager as always to learn a new English word.

"No-one you know," Lenny answered.

Alex told him that it was just an expression.

"Bum," said Lenny. "Rhyming slang. Cockney."

"Not on – your knee?" Yianis looked puzzled by Lenny's bark of laughter.

"No," said Alex. "Breath. Nelly, smelly, smelly breath, breath of life. So not on my life."

"Trust you to know," put in Lenny. His grin was so wide in his freckled face that his eyes all but disappeared.

"I know it's a little complicated," Alex carried on, conscious that he was being pedantic, even about such a trivial thing. He left them with a wave of his hand. What a strange life. Tonight they might be killing Germans. This morning they were laughing in the sun.

The chapel was little more than a hut built of stones from the surrounding land, but it did have an arched doorway surmounted by a carved wooden cross painted white. Inside, light came from a small window at the far end and there was a rough wooden screen half-hiding the altar. It held a crude painting of St George slaying the dragon. There was also a circular stand set with thimble-shaped holders for candles. Alex found a collection of new tapers in a wall alcove and a box of matches.

He had lit a taper and was about to set it in a holder on the stand when the door creaked open.

"Aleko!"

He turned swiftly and dropped the candle.

"Ileana!"

They both bent to pick it up at the same moment but sprang apart, bounding backwards as though from an electric shock. Their eyes locked in silent question. Then they both spoke, Ileana first.

"Sorry!"

"Sorry!"

"I did not know you were here."

"Neither did I. I mean, I didn't know. I mean, I didn't think." But he was thinking about her, all the time.

Ileana told him she'd seen him from a distance, making for the chapel.

"Yes," he said. A nonsensical affirmation.

"I had to see you."

"I came here to find you."

"We musn't."

"I know. But we must."

They were in each other's arms. Alex pulled off Ileana's scarf and buried his face in her hair, tilting her head back, finding her mouth with his. She was trying to speak, protesting feebly, she could not do this, her life was here, he would leave, people would find out, she needed to be married to Nikos, she had nothing, she needed to be safe, Alex had a wife, he'd leave. Her black eyelashes gleamed with tears. He stopped her mouth with his. Her words were as nothing, their bodies commanded silence, they were united in a way which allowed neither past nor future. They were alive, now.

Later, they decided they should go down to the cave separately in case anyone saw them. Alex would go first; then Ileana with the tureen of stew in the basket she'd left outside the chapel.

When she entered the cave half an hour later, Alex had his head down. He was occupied with preparing two explosive charges. "Nobel's 808," he told Yiannis who was watching him intently. "One would do the job, but two to be certain."

"Certain," repeated Yiannis.

Alex was acutely aware of Ileana's close presence as she doled out the stew. They all sat on the ground outside the cave to eat the meal. They were unusually silent. There was no argument, no discussion, no banter. Alex thought he should relieve the tension in some way, but he was too tense himself, not only on account of the coming mission but also because of his preoccupation with Ileana. He also had to come to a decision about Nikos – to include him in the team or not.

After the meal, he didn't go down to the river to help her with the plates. This was remarked upon, by Lenny and also by Philipas and Lefteris.

"Not today," he told. "I'm going to have a good, long siesta."

Soon all the men who'd go with Alex that night were lying down in the cave, some sleeping lightly, others snoring heavily or remaining fretfully wideawake despite determinedly closed eyes.

Alex didn't sleep but stayed awake, wrapped in amazed, step-by-step recollection of his time with Ileana. He promised himself he'd treasure it for as long as he lived but he would never repeat it. He had no regrets, no feeling at all that he'd been unfaithful to Joan. He was certain that if she ever found out, she'd understand the reason why he had to live to the full on this day. It might be his last.

The men woke at sunset and spent the next hours in restless preparation. The ones chosen for the operation were all allowed a single shot of *tsipouro* before they set off. Nikos was still under the impression he was part of it and queued up for the drink. Alex knew he had managed this badly. It was inexcusable to be so unclear. He now had to decide to include or exclude Niko.

There was no concrete reason to suspect Nikos of unreliability but there'd been many moments when he'd caught an expression of watchful suspicion on Niko's face. He hadn't wanted to put this down to his own easy friendship with Ileana. He had dismissed from his mind any acknowledgment that he was infringing the local code of conduct. He had until now believed in the innocence of his own behaviour. After all, he himself was not Greek, not local.

But he was no longer innocent. In fact, to be truthful, he never had been.

Slowly Alex realised that, although he didn't feel guilty towards Joan, he'd always felt guilty towards Nikos and this was what fed his imagination. Nikos must be intensely jealous, so he'd be justified in taking revenge. In that case, he must be given no opportunity to do so. He musn't be anywhere near explosive material or gunfire. At the same time, he must be included otherwise he would have another reason to hate Alex. Yes, it was hate that Alex saw in his eyes.

With ten minutes to go before leaving the cave, a solution came to him. He'd give Nikos a role that included him in the team but kept him safely away from the action.

"Oh Niko, by the way," he said, calling him aside before they set off. "I've been thinking. I want you to take a vital position on our return route. You know the big boulder at the beginning of the bandits' trail up the mountain? That's your station. You'll be on your own, and I shall depend on you to cover our retreat." Had he put this well enough in Greek? He added, "*Endaxi?*" with a definite question mark.

"*Endaxi*," came the reply.

Okay. All in order. Alex felt relieved.

The tramp down the river was easier this time, although they were carrying more equipment, and they arrived at the old arched bridge before three o'clock in the morning. It took a few minutes to blacken-up: faces were smeared with ash, and black gloves and balaclavas, which had been knitted by the village women, were pulled on. The men were in a state of nervous excitement, which Alex tried to calm. He gave up in the end, thinking this was a better state to be in than silent dread, which could be paralysing.

He sent three men across to the far side of the river. They were to hide in a culvert not far from the two parked vehicles to provide the same sort of distraction and cover as Byron and Lefteris were to do on Alex's side of the river. Nikos was sent off to take up position at the start of the bandits' trail. Thanos, Yiannis and Alex himself proceeded slowly along the river bank towards the bridge, moving ahead each time the guards wheeled about. After watching for a while, Alex came to the conclusion that the patrol on duty was the one that had been described as slacker than the others. Each time the soldiers met in the middle of the bridge, they paused for at least a minute, continuing a conversation which as far as Alex could make out referred to the mixed fortunes of a regimental football team.

He nodded to Thanos and Yiannis and they entered the river, wading carefully to the chosen position. A great calm came over Alex. He'd prepared well. His two helpers knew exactly what to do, handing him the tools he needed, precisely when he needed them and without a fumble. Each step was accomplished smoothly: first fixing the charge, the insertion of the yellow lozenge, the plastic 808, then tamping it in, followed by a section of wood to hold it in place; finally, checking the connection to the length of wire, before slowly backing away, unwinding the roll of wire as he did so. This was the most difficult part. The detonator had to be placed securely on the bank, far enough away for safety, near enough to be out of sight of the patrol. There was no such position. Alex had to place the detonator rather nearer the bridge than he would have liked. Yiannis, understanding the difficulty, tapped his chest. Alex understood he was offering to be the one to set off the detonator. He was fast and sure-footed. It made sense. He could get out of the way and join the others on the bandit trail far more quickly than Alex.

Alex shook his head and then changed the movement to a very definite Greek no, raising his head and closing his eyes. For good measure, he put his hand on Yiannis's back and gave him a good push. The two men, father and son, loped away, doubled-up in the shadow of the bank.

Alex gave them a moment. He rested his back against the bank and looked up at the sky. The slip of moon was near the horizon and the morning star was shining. A soft breath of air brought the smell of waterweed. The river seemed to hold a song. A moment of perfection which he was about to destroy with one finger. He pressed the detonator, scrambled to his feet and ran. He had twenty seconds, he reckoned. He could do it.

Halfway to the boulder at the foot of the trail, the land lit up around him in a colossal white star. He didn't hear the explosion. He didn't need to. His mission was done. He knew everything was as it should be when he saw Nikos rise behind the boulder with his rifle to his eye.

The bullet slammed into his skull through the centre of his forehead and in the white light her name sounded, each letter a note of music in a descending scale, the syllables like perfect tears falling as he fell, back into the river.

PART TWO

The present day

II CHAPTER ONE

I was five years old when I learnt that Thomas was not my father.

I was playing with – correction - I was *looking after* the twins in the sandpit Thomas had built for us – correction – *them*, in a corner of the apple orchard. They were not quite three at the time.

Me: "Don't do that!"

John continued to pour sand down the back of Jeanie's dress

"John!"

He paid no attention until I said "I'll tell Daddy!"

Then it came. "He's not your Daddy." John had a weird expression on his face, slightly twisted as though he was sucking a lemon. He wanted to get back at me.

"No," said Jeanie in her lispy little girl voice which she never grew out of. She knew her little girl voice was considered sweet. "No, ee'th not your Daddee." She looked gleeful, even if she had no idea of the import of what she was saying.

The chill went straight through me. I put up a protest for a while but I knew at once this was the truth. It made absolute sense of all the small, vague moments, hesitations, things not said, things avoided. Much, much later, Joan gave me the reason they'd delayed telling me. They thought I was too young to know that my father had been shot – and that means killed - by the Germans in the war.

I was never too young for that knowledge. Facts of such far-reaching potency should be told to new human beings well before they can really understand. Then it is never a shock, it is simply absorbed and they never have to dismantle a false belief.

Joan still maintains that she was going to tell me on my sixth birthday. She repeats herself frequently about many of the major events in her life. The minor, too. The fact that she was going to tell me about Alex she repeats whenever prompted by the thought of a birthday. Anyone's birthday, not necessarily mine. Perhaps she feels bad that she married Thomas so soon after my birth.

When I learnt Thomas was not my father, I began calling him Tom. At the same time, I started calling Joan *Joan,* rather than Mummy. Perhaps I felt, at some level, that she'd let me down. I was resentful. As though she'd kept my real father from me.

I needed to know about him, but there was so little she could tell me. On the sandpit day I'd gone straight in to find her in the kitchen.

"Have I got two daddies?"

She looked shocked and tearful. She explained as best she could. My first daddy was a hero. He died in the war.

Over the years, I was drip-fed scraps of knowledge to put together. I'd ask Joan important questions every so often, but I knew not to press for answers. I'd choose my moment.

She called him Alex although his full name was Alexander. His surname was Pritchard. She and Thomas had changed my name to Pike when I started school. The Pritchards lived in Wales. They were my grandparents but not like my Colebrook Farm grandparents. *Why don't my Alex grandparents send birthday cards? Because we are not in touch.* That led to another why, which had only recently been asked and answered.

As I grew older, my questions became more sophisticated. Living on a farm, I knew that there was a lapse of time between mating and birth. Lambs were born five months after the ram was allowed in with the ewes. I needed to know how long it took humans to be made. *How long were you and Alex married? Not nearly long enough.*

I think I'd gone away to boarding school before I'd straightened out the timetable. Alex was killed by the Germans on October 15th 1943.I was born on April 18th 1944.The last time Alex had been at Colebrook Farm had been the summer of 1943. *When exactly? Oh, Helen, for goodness sake. You know it's painful for me.*

I learnt to live with the lack of knowledge. The bare facts were enough. At school I was not unusual. There were other girls who'd lost a father in the war, which was the phrase we used, making the war sound like a dense fog. I could imagine all these poor soldiers stumbling around with their hands held out in the front of them. We never talked about what the loss might mean for us. Our conversations dealt with the all-consuming topics of the moment, like who had been chosen to play Gwendoline in The Importance of Being Earnest.

It was only the other day that I learnt how very little time Joan and Alex had spent together.

I'd gone to visit Joan at Colebrook. I try and see Joan regularly – you never know with someone in their late 90s how much longer they'll be around. Joan's doing well. Although she can barely see – she's had macular degeneration for years - and she needs hearing aids, she is healthy and can still walk as far as the orchard. She takes her stick and a basket to collect any eggs she finds under the hedge. It's amazing what she can see out of the corner of her eye.

She made a pot of tea and we sat opposite each other at her kitchen table. She enjoys talking about the old days, recounting oft-repeated stories of farm and family. "That was when ---" is always the introduction to some such memory. She was well into one such reminiscence when she gave me – unwittingly, I expect – an unexpected opening.

"That was the last time I saw your father," she said, pushing a plate of flapjack towards me.

"Last time?"

"Yes, his last leave."

"The summer before I was born."

"Mmm."

"It must have been July."

"It probably was."

"Did he often get leave?"

"Oh no, I don't think so."

"Don't think so? How often did you see each other?"

Joan was adding sugar to her tea and spoke very softly. "I didn't know him very well."

"Sorry. I missed that. What did you say?"

"We didn't know each other very long."

And then it came out. They'd met at a party in London. He'd visited her in Devon. They'd got married and had a few days' honeymoon in Cornwall. His next leave was his last. All happened within a month.

"In the war, we were all in a hurry."

I could understand that. None of us know when we are going to face death. In wartime, the pressure to do what we can when we can is even greater.

I need to learn more about my father while I can. That's why I'm on this bus, heading for Glikopigi.

II CHAPTER TWO

Glikopigi. Sweet spring of water. When as a teenager I learnt from Joan that this was the name of the place where my father had been killed, I was enchanted. It gave me the notion that the ground where he'd fallen was hallowed, as though a priest had sprinkled holy water on it. I know that's fanciful. The spot may now be a village tip. But Sweet Spring it has been for me since I learnt the meaning of the name when I was living in Athens as a young au pair.

I realise, as I hear the vigorous chorus of Greek voices in the bus, that I am completing something I began in that first year in Greece – the search for my father. The realisation surprises me. I wasn't conscious of any particular motive at the time. I simply wanted to go abroad, and do something other than knuckle down to nine-to-five office work. I replied to an advertisement in the Times personal column: *au pair wanted for Greek-American family in Athens*. I gave in my notice at the estate agency I'd joined a year before, and jumped on what later became known as the Magic Bus which took people like me - looking for adventure without much money – across Europe to Greece. I certainly knew that my father had been killed in the war in that country, but I didn't think for a moment I was tracking him, in the way I am now. He was something sealed away in the past, untouchable. But once living with the family – a couple of busy journalists, with two quite difficult children - I set my mind on learning the language. I continued learning when I returned to England and took up my job again at Halberts. A Greek language teacher in Exeter has kept my conversational abilities from rusting away to nothing.

The reasons for the choices we make are not always clear at the time; years down the line, we see how natural they were and how well they fit in with our life's trajectory. Or is that a chicken-and-egg situation? The choices we make create the trajectory. Speaking the language certainly helped Richard and me when we were sailing around the islands. But I never thought I would return to Greece and find the mountains in the north where my father was shot and killed. Our life revolved around the yacht, kept in Greek waters for summer sun and sea. Only as a widow, with only myself to take into account, did I decide on this trip. I'm now ready for it.

"But Mum, on your own?" Rachel's voice was full of doubt. (She thinks I'm not safe to be let out). "Why not join a group?" She found a mass of information for me on the internet. "Here's a good one. *An off-the-beaten track itinerary. Explore the Pindos, 10 days for £1399 per person including flights.*"

"I don't want to explore the Pindos. I simply want to stand on the very spot where my father fell."

Rachel's forehead did its familiar trick of imitating corrugated cardboard.

In a way, Rachel was right to query my decision to visit Glikopigi on my own. Not that I'm in the slightest bit fearful of travelling solo. Rather, my trepidation is prompted by the thought of what I may discover. Going by Joan's reluctance to talk about the past, I guess the villagers of Glikopigi may not want to be reminded of the war and the civil war. I know enough about the horrors of those years through my reading. In fact, I've brought the paperback of John Gage's Eleni with me to re-read. That's the moving story of an American journalist tracking the perpetrators of his Greek mother's murder. Mine is a different story. My questions won't uncover a murder; there's no reason to be fearful. Still, I might not have made the journey had it not been for a conversation in the spring with my granddaughter. She told me she was booked for a fortnight in Greece in July. Holly, not that you'd guess it by looking at her fringed waistcoats, short, lace-hemmed dresses, high boots and all the bits of silver she threads through lips, nostrils, earlobes and who knows what else, is an archaeology student at Bristol. She was going to be with a group of students, on a dig.

"Greece! How exciting! Where?"

"A cave somewhere north of Yannina."

"Oh yes, where exactly?"

"We get mini-bussed to a village an hour away called, oh, glockenspiegel or something."

"That's German!" Strange how it jarred.

Holly looked shocked by my response. It wasn't possible to explain that I didn't want to hear the sound of that language in connection with Greece.

The village where the students would be based turned out to be Glikopigi. Sometimes one has to wonder whether there isn't some previously designed network underlying the surface of our lives. Threads get tweaked every now again to pull us up short or connect us, one with another. Meet someone briefly when you're 23 and be prepared to come across them again the other side of the world when you're 60. Holly was going to be close to the place where my father, her great grandfather, was killed by the Germans in the Second World War. She expressed polite but distant interest. A great grandfather is irrelevant, neither not far enough in the past nor close enough to the present. Her period is Paleolithic. For me, though, the coincidence was the clincher. Not that I will get in her way, she'll be involved with her fellow diggers, but it will be nice to have her around. She's a very calm, soothing sort of person and we've always been close. Rachel was reasssured to think that her mother and her daughter would be together. She immediately took over the research into transport. She's an inveterate arranger of holidays and is always googling.

So, two days ahead of Holly, here I am in Greece again, having landed in Corfu yesterday. The low approach over the sea induced the remembered rush of terror. You cannot believe there is enough land to land on. Richard and I used to hold hands, our grip growing tighter as the plane lost height. Preveza was the airport we used more often. We preferred to draw up the boat for the winter in Vliho on the island of Lefkadha. The boatyard there was our favourite; the sailing and anchorages in coves around the neighbouring islands are many and glorious. If we landed at Corfu, it was a matter of heading straight down to Lefkadha, a waste of precious days. Neither of us took long holidays in the summer. That's the key time people want to sell, look at and buy houses.

Now I have all the time in the world − a state I would have welcomed when Richard was alive. Yesterday, I felt a conflicting rush of emotions. I was happy to feel the heat of the sun, hear the language, read the Greek signs in the arrival hall but none of these pleasures could dispel the tide of sadness that engulfed me. I miss Richard all the time but mostly it's just a background ache. It's at times like these that his absence hits me in the solar plexus afresh. There's nobody to share responses with. Just look at the sunset, I wanted to say on the ferry across to Igoumenitsa. What sort of place has Rachel booked us into? Correction: booked *me* into.

It was clean and comfortable and conveniently near the bus station. Trust Rachel. She also worked out bus times and connections. But − here's another sudden realisation − this is the wrong bus. It's trundling off the main road to villages up in the hills. Too late now. This will be a long journey to Yannina. Never mind.

There are lot of empty seats. Mine is sticking to me in the searing heat. Sticky-backed plastic, I think, remembering Blue Peter with the children. I'm just behind the driver. He's called Costa and he's 40, married with two children. There, you see: we're in a typical conversation already. He knows my age and that I'm a widow. Soon he'll want to know where I'm going and why. I shall talk about Holly. Yes! I knew she'd be a useful shield. People in Glikopigi will understand that I'm there to keep an eye on my granddaughter. I needn't talk about my father and the war until I've been there long enough to gauge reactions. I have a month, and could extend it if that seems like a good idea.

Right now, it does seem like a good idea. I'm enjoying looking at the scenery, past the view of Costa's wide shoulders, the plastic flowers, pictures of saints, and beads strung about the windscreen in front of him.

Costa is a hairy man. His neck, front and back and all the way around, is covered in thick black, curly hair which disappears into his white shirt. I imagine it completely covers his torso. What makes him keep his face clean-shaven, yet leave his neck hair to grow? The contrast at jawline between smooth skin above and matted curls below is striking. A kind of upside down picture. In my mind's eye I give him a black beard bushing out either side of his head below his ears. He becomes a children's book pirate.

"So – are you staying in Yannina?" He half turns to address me, shouting above the noise of the engine. "My cousin can find you a room. Very good hotel, down by the lake. Very clean, very comfortable."

His shoulders don't exactly slump when I don't take up the offer, but he's clearly disappointed. I cheer him up. "I'm going on to Glikopigi. Do you know anyone there?"

Costa doesn't but the woman sitting across the aisle becomes animated. Her brother-in-law runs a taverna there which has rooms. She scrabbles in her big, black handbag for a card. "Right in the middle, near the church," she tells me. "Ask for Michalakis's guest house."

I take the card. A four-legged animal is holding up a sign with the name Michalakis written on it in decorative script. "Oh! Is that a ---?" I leave the question hanging in the air, not wanting to hazard a guess. A relation may well have drawn the creature.

"Yes. A bear. There are bears in the mountains."

I'm thrilled. It may turn out to be like Yosemite where we camped with the children when they were young teenagers. A bear came in the night – or so we learnt in the washhouse in the morning – and ransacked the contents of a hold-all someone had left outside a tent. There was a trail of torn bags and wrapping foil leading away into the trees.

Harry and Rachel wanted to follow the trail, but we wouldn't let them. Their howls of protest were half-hearted. They were still at the age of obeying us.

"Do they come down to the village?" I ask my new friend across the aisle.

"They come for the cherries just as they're ripening. They climb up and strip the trees. None for us!"

"They break branches," says a voice from further behind me. "Ruin the trees."

"When's that?"

"End of May, early June. Don't worry. You won't see a bear now it's August."

More voices join in. There's a lively conversation about bears and wolves in the mountains. And goats, wild ones. Everyone wants to explain to me what they mean

85

by wild goats. An athletic-looking, young man comes and squats in the aisle beside me. He describes the animal by holding his index fingers crooked backwards over his head.

"It's a protected animal," he says before lowering his voice to add, "but it does taste very good." He gives me a winning smile, a flash of white teeth in a tanned face. Greek men can be very good-looking. If I were half my age ...

I think of Richard, with a small, sad, internal smile. A Greek rule is made to be broken, he used to say, enjoying the phenomenon when it suited him, laughing at it when he wasn't affected by it, disparaging it at other times. How many orange groves don't exist, he'd ask when a conversation turned to the EU. But he loved riding a hired motorbike without a helmet, driving a car without doing up the safety belt, avoiding customs duty when we kept the boat in Greek waters longer than the allotted length of time --- that was a rule we broke with guilty pleasure, or pleasurable guilt. We went to elaborate lengths to pretend we were off to Italy for a short trip. We signed out from one port, bid the Customs Officer adieu, hid in a remote cove for the length of time it would take to cross to Italy and back, and sailed into a different port with expressions of relief to have avoided the worst of an imagined gale. We could hardly take the moral high ground where rule-breaking was concerned.

The backward-pointing horns indicated by the young man give me the clue. "*Chamois?*" I say in English. "We call wild goat *chamois*."

"Ah, she's English," I hear from the row behind me.

"What's she doing going to Yannina?"

"Is she on her own?"

My new friend across the aisle raises her voice above the others. She wants to know how it is I can speak Greek. I tell her of my Athens year as a young woman, followed by the years of family sailing. This provokes more questions.

The bus rolls on. We exchange names. Calliope comes to sit beside me. I squeeze up to the window to allow her warm, comfortable body enough room. She's dressed in black, with a black headscarf loosely draped over her head. She's a widow, too. We turn out, to our mutual surprise, to be the same age. I've been placing her nearer Joan's generation.

I know we make an odd pair. I'm conscious of my thin, jean-clad legs, my denim shirt open over a sleeveless blue top which is little more than a band across my minimal breasts, my overlong back pressed into the window corner, my funny old face topped by a mass of grey hair as hard to comb as a Brillo pad – and my feet in galumphing great hiking boots, bought especially for this trip. We're two elderly women sharing a bus journey but what different lives have led us to this point. I realise, with a start of surprise, that Calliope would have lived through the tail end of the German occupation and the years of civil war. The thought makes me tense for a moment. *Ghosts.* I give a little shiver to shake them off.

While Calliope talks of her many successful grandchildren, I keep glancing out of the window. The road passes close to the Mourgana mountains where Nicolas Gage's mother Eleni lived and died. I'm on the look-out for recognisable names on signposts. When I spot a sign to Filiates, I find I've read it aloud. It's the nearest town to the village of Lia.

Calliope turns towards me with surprise. "Does it mean something to you?"

"Oh no, no!"

"They made a film there, you know. A film about the difficult years."

I risk asking her if she knows the area. She doesn't. I am relieved, as I don't feel up to hearing at first-hand about anything that happened in these mountains in the civil war. My father's time and place were different.

Calliope is saying something about her childhood. It sounds as though her family were shepherds. They used to take their sheep from the plains around Igoumenitsa where they'd spent the winter, and up to the Pindos mountains for the summer. "Rich grass up there," she tells me. "My father had the grazing rights on a high plateau above the village where you're staying."

"Oh! Near Glikopigi?"

"Well yes. And the Tesserahoria."

The four villages? It's beginning to sound like a bigger, more populated area than I ever imagined.

My imagination has had precious little to work with. Really, it's only been fed by the few bits of information from Joan, and the contents of the small leather folder she let me have when I was 16.

"Your turn to look after this," she said, handing it over. I think it had been a desk blotter once, or something of that sort. Purply-blue leather with two black ribbons that held the two covers together. Inside were loose papers: my father's birth certificate, his army record, a War Office telegram announcing his death, newspaper cuttings from The Exeter Express and Echo and the Times - *heroic action, leading his men, valuable service in the field* – and the photograph I've kept beside me ever since. It's in my bag right now. Alex is leaning on the gate into the orchard, and looking at the camera with an expression I'd describe as lazy and loving. ("His last leave, just think", says Joan). It's a black and white photograph that's been tinted with colour ("Old Mr Porter did that, you know the photography shop near Dingles?"). He has fair, army-cut hair but there's a lock that's slipped down over his forehead. ("Yes, it really annoyed me the way he kept pushing it back, but he wouldn't let me snip it short"). He is in army uniform, with a captain's pips on his shoulder. Joan was proud of him. Young to be made a captain. Too young to be killed.

I want to show the photograph to Calliope so I get it from my bag.

"My father," I say. "He was killed in the war somewhere near Glikopigi."

"Oh, *Panayia mou.*" She crosses herself three times. "I am sincerely sorry. You must miss him terribly."

"No. I can't miss someone I never knew."

"Oh but your *father.*"

"I am curious about him, certainly. That's why I'm here."

Yet, even as I speak, I know I'm not being strictly accurate. You can miss a father you never knew.

II CHAPTER THREE

On the left of the road, the land drops steeply away to a river with wide, pebbly shores. In winter it's probably a wild torrent of water coming down from the distant mountains.

"Mourgana?" I ask Calliope. She nods but wants to get back to telling me of her grandchildren's successes.

I have the idea that Lia is up there in one of the smoke-grey folds, blurred by heat haze and distance. Nicolas Gage's mother Eleni, her legs swollen from beatings, shuffled on bare feet up that mountain. She was one of thirteen prisoners led to the terraced field where they were shot, their lifeless bodies tumbling into the mass grave dug ready for them. This terrible image haunts me.

I read the book, and others about the war years, after Richard died. His death somehow removed whatever obstacle had stopped me, until then, from exploring the context of my father's death. Perhaps bereavement allows us to let in our grief at earlier losses. Yet, as I've just told Calliope, I've never mourned my father. His absence wasn't a loss in that way. I wept for weeks over Richard. And I wept for nine-year-old Nicolas and his mother, Eleni. She saved him from being sent by the communists to Albania – and was tortured and executed while he and his sisters escaped for life in America. The tragic loss of a mother by a son, and the loss of a son by a mother, catches me without fail.

Calliope has been asking me something. "Sorry?"

"Family. Tell me about your family. It's your turn!"

I start with Harry. He and Megan took their three boys to live in Vancouver years ago. As I describe my middle-aged and absent son, it strikes me that he could be the wellspring of my tears over Eleni. I hurry on to talk of Rachel and Hugh and their only child, Holly.

Calliope is pleased to hear they live near me. "My daughter, too, lives close," she says. "In the same apartment block in Yannina."

"Wonderful."

"She's the mother of the girl who is studying in Italy." Calliope is back talking about her own family just when I was geared up to boast about Holly. I sink into my corner and let the talk wash over me.

Yannina bus station, three hours later.

I'm back among the crowds having spent the afternoon flat out under a pine tree in a park. With my head on my backpack, I slept well despite a few furry caterpillars which I flicked away every so often. Richard and I on our city breaks would often lie down for a quick nap in suitably grassy places. This is the first time I've done such a thing on my own – well, not since I was young, free and unattached between school and marriage. There is a marked difference now, though. I feel more relaxed. No-one's going to bother an old woman like me. Another not so welcome difference: I ached all over when I struggled to my feet.

The bus to Glikopigi is being boarded, so I join the queue. I'm no longer the odd one out. There are others with backpacks and hiking boots and I can hear a number of languages being spoken: French, German, American, possibly Polish or Russian. Will I be staying in the midst of a tourist hotspot? How will this affect my aim of delving into the second world war?

Why didn't I hire a car, they asked me on the bus from Igoumenitsa. Foreigners hire cars. Why not me? The answer that half-satisfied my interrogators was that I couldn't afford it. I shall be here for a month or longer. But it's not just the expense. I don't want to seal myself away in a tin box. I want to be in direct contact with whatever happens, not put at one remove by a car or a husband.

Calliope on the previous bus asked me what my late husband, *God rest his soul*, had done in his working life. I'd forgotten the word I'd learnt in the past so I described as best I could the business of an estate agent and surveyor. "It was a family firm. I'd joined it as a secretary straight from college. Married the son of the boss. In the end, we were joint partners."

Calliope was impressed. "Bravo, Eleni," she said.

Recalling this, as I queue for the Glikopigi bus, I hear again the name she called me. Of course! This is what I am called in Greece.

Before I heave my rucksack into the bowels of the bus, I find a pack of damp tissues and take it onto the bus. Is the outbreak of itchiness on the back of my neck caused by the sudden shifts I'm experiencing between past and present?

Prickly heat, I hear Richard tell me. He was always bringing me down to earth.

I wipe my face and neck. The fragrant, cool dampness is a relief. The girl who has come to sit beside me looks as hot as I feel.

I hand her the packet and watch as she takes a wipe and buries her face in it. Her pony tail swings as she looks up at me with a broad smile.

"Danke schon."

We fall into conversation, a mixture of her halting English and my school-level German. It feels the wrong language to be speaking on the bus taking me up into the mountains where Germans were my father's enemy. But I chide myself. That was then. Now is now. Besides, several of us opted to learn German at school, despite the war being in the relatively recent past, and all the girls were daughters of army officers.

The girl whose name is Heidi is about Holly's age. She holds her phone in the same way, her bent thumbs poised to tap out a message to a friend. *On the bus! Too hot!* The same need to report every second of experience. Can't blame her. It's what I'm doing myself.

We've been climbing away from the low ground beyond the town of Yannina. It's not unlike being in a plane, looking down on the chequerboard of irrigated fields. Heidi points out a hump of rocky land. "The cave of stalactites. You have seen?"

"No. I only arrived yesterday. Perhaps on my return."

"How long you stay in Tesserahori?"

"Where?" It takes a second to make out the single name for the group of four villages, as described by Calliope on the previous bus. "Oh no, I'm going to Glikopigi."

Heidi and her group will be staying in the smallest village of the four, Mikro Kipseli. "We will walk the gorge to tomorrow," she tells me. "Eleven kilometres."

"Interessante," I say. That sounds more Italian than German. Have I got it wrong?

Heidi has a map in her shoulder bag which she shows me. It's a hand drawn, photocopied map of the mountain range with lettering I can't read. My spectacles are in my rucksack.

"Tesserahori," she says, with her index finger on one side of the map. "And here is the gorge." Her finger traces a wiggly line at the bottom of the page. She points to the opposite side.

I peer at the map. There are dotted lines connecting the villages and a dotted line along the gorge. Dotted line equals footpath; I know this well from Dartmoor walking maps. There's no sign of a road between Tesserahori and Glikopigi.

It takes a minute or two before I accept that I'm on the wrong bus.

How has this happened? I cast my mind back to the day Holly, Rachel and I sat around the kitchen table with glasses of Merlot. We were working out when and where Holly and I would meet up. Holly and her group would be staying in a hostel in the village. I'd be in a guesthouse Rachel had found. She enjoys trawling the internet. Flight, dates and where to stay I left her to fix. The rest – the ferry, the buses - was general guidance, written down in her neat writing. So where had I gone wrong?

I recall Holly's voice.

"Glikopigi is one of four villages on the slopes of the mountain." She said it firmly, with great authority.

"Yes," said Rachel. "When you arrive in Yannina you'll have a few hours to wait. Have a meal or something." She passed a map of the town across the table, with the bus station ringed in yellow. "There's a bus at 5 and another at 6. Better get the earlier one," she told me.

You know that feeling - the ground's been taken from under you. The lift's gone down and left you in the air.

I turn back to Heidi. "Could I look at that map again?" I'm reluctant to think that my lovely granddaughter, young, bright Holly, made a mistake. But Heidi's map is clear. There are four villages on the southern slopes of the mountain. I ask Heidi to read out the names. Mikro Kipseli, Kato Kipseli, Meso Kipseli, Ano Kipseli. There are four Kipseli's from little to lower, middle and higher. And, on the far side of the mountain massif, Glikopigi. Worse, there is absolutely no sign of a connecting road, however hard I look at the map.

Ano Kipseli

I let everyone else get off the bus first. When no-one is left on board, I join the driver who is unloading the last few items of baggage. I still entertain a faint hope so I ask the question which I know is dumb. "Are you going on to Glikopigi?"

"Ha! You want me to drive on sheep trails?" He's laughing at me. He turns to a tall, grey-haired man helping offload the luggage. "This little English lady wants me to drive her across the mountain!" There's some appreciative laughter in the group of locals hanging around the bus. A lively discussion starts about my best course of action.

There are many suggestions. Heidi has already invited me to join the group on tomorrow's hike. But eleven kilometres of gorge and then a long climb to Glikopigi with my rucksack is beyond me, although I'm pleased that she should consider me capable of it. The only way by road gives me the choice. I can return to Yannina right now, and stay the night there before catching the morning bus to Glikopigi. Or I can stay the night here and return to Yannina in the morning to wait for the afternoon bus. I'm exhausted after all the travelling and look around for a possible night's stay. We're in what looks like a quarry with a number of parked cars. The elderly man reaches for my rucksack. "Come with me," he says and strides off towards some steps leading up into what I guess is the village. I follow thankfully. It's good to be in Greece where I feel able to trust a stranger.

II CHAPTER FOUR

Someone is addressing me. A polite enquiry. "May I?"

I look up from the thin and flyblown paperback I found in a pile on a windowsill inside the taverna. Its title attracted me. *Hidden Gold in the Pindos Mountains, a first-hand account of a post-war adventure, by Leonard Milligan.* I'm hoping this will turn out to be about the gold sovereigns that were dropped into Greece to fund the resistance, but I haven't got beyond the title page. Matheos, the grandson of the elderly man who led me here, has brought more wine to the table and another glass.

"Certainly!"

He sits down.

"How was the meal?"

"Excellent." I can be truthful. A wonderful *stifadho* with little onions in a thick tomato sauce.

"You like the wine?"

I nod with just the right amount of vigour. Sometimes it's best not to be truthful.

"It's from our own grapes."

That explains it. Richard and I learnt to avoid homemade wines.

"I didn't think that at this height ...?"

"Oh no, we have a vineyard in Thessaly."

"You're not from here then?" In our last few years sailing, we noticed people came to tourist hotspots from all over Greece to set up businesses. They were cannier at making profits than the locals. It was probably the same situation here.

"My wife is."

Oh, so he'd married into the village. Not a complete outsider then.

I'm sitting at one of several tables outside the taverna in the main flag-stoned square. Heidi and her group have eaten and departed. I shall go to bed myself very soon, but Matheos is keen to tell me about the locality. The village is the centre for hikers, he says. People come from all over the world. There's a small museum. The village is far superior to the others on the slopes of the mountain.

"Glikopigi is nothing. You must stay here. Here we have foreigners who have rebuilt ruins." He pauses for admiration but I can't express any interest. I'm retired from house buying and selling, and I'm on the wrong side of the mountain for my present purpose.

"Australians," he adds, as though this will persuade me to stay. "Imagine, they come all the way from the other side of the world to spend the summer here."

An old man sitting at the next table breaks in. "Eh, Matheo! They're from *London!*" I have the idea from his expression – dancing eyes under furrowed brow – that he likes correcting Matheos.

"Okay. But originally from Australia, *pappou.*"

Is the old man another grandfather – or is Matheos using *pappou* as a term of familiarity tinged with respect.

"No! Not Australia. New Zealand! They're Kiwis!" *Pappou* uses the English word, drawing out the eee sounds. "From *London.*"

Matheos turns to me, tossing his head and closing his eyes. He's implying that the old man is a bit gaga.

Pappou leans across and taps the flyblown book I'd begun to read. "The man who wrote this was here in the German war."

Now I am one hundred per cent interested. I urge the old man to continue.

He does so, after a brief coughing fit. "I was a small boy and I remember him well. He came back after the war." Pappou goes silent.

Oh, don't dry up on me. "And bought a ruin?" I prompt.

"No, no. That was later. His son. In the 1980s. His son was a surgeon in a London hospital. It's the surgeon's family who comes here. They're here now. You must meet them."

I don't go along with the '*must*'. They are too far removed from my area of interest.

"I'll come back another time," I say. "I'm meeting my granddaughter in Glikopigi." I explain about Holly's archaeological excavations. "I must catch the bus back to Yannina in the morning."

Matheos and Pappou reluctantly accept Holly as my reason for leaving their village so quickly. Matheos says I can take the book to read at my leisure and give it back when I visit again. "It's our only copy but you're welcome to borrow it. That way, you have to come back to Ano Kipseli." What a practised charmer. He's making me feel half my age.

Glikopigi

Another bus. Another day. My feet are insufferably hot in my boots. It was Rachel who persuaded me to bring them. She said I'd need them in the mountains and it

94

was best to wear them on the journey, rather than pack such heavy items and anyway I wouldn't have the room in the backpack she advised me to bring instead of a suitcase. Why do I listen to my daughter? I should have brought a suitcase and hired a car.

But I am getting close. We've long since passed a sign to Tesserahori. We've also passed a turning to the Albanian border. The man sitting next to me has pointed out a feature on a hill to the left of the road north. Large white painted stones spell out Oχι. That was what the Greek Prime Minister said in 1940 when the Italians assumed they could simply walk in and take over Greece. No, said Ioannis Metaxas, they couldn't. A bitter war in freezingly cold winter weather followed. My bus companion describes all this with careful patience. He was at first surprised that I was so ignorant, even though – as he said – my ability to speak Greek was so good. Beta class, he said, Alpha being beginners' halting Greek, and Gamma being five-star fluency.

Perhaps by the time I leave I'll have reached Gamma. I'm getting enough practice.

The bus is slowly climbing a zigzag road which every so often allows a glimpse of high peaks, pinkish-grey and pale in the distance. The hillsides are covered in scrub and low shrubs growing between white and terracotta coloured rocks. A flock of goats is driven across the road, and the bus driver waits for the last few animals to skitter down the red earth embankment, scattering stones on the road before they cross and disappear down the opposite side. The goatherd, a very young boy – about ten? - watches us go past, examining with intent every passenger. What sort of life, I wonder, lies before him. I cannot guess.

My neighbour is talking about the common market. I know that Greece is in desperate debt but now I learn more details. They want to crucify us, he says. He fulminates against a number of groups of people; I'm not at all sure who these are. I just understand that my companion wants to send them all to hell. "We should never have let them back in," he says. I make out that these "them" are the communists who had been banished after the civil war but were granted amnesty by the left-wing government and had returned from the Soviet bloc in the more recent past.

The man in front of my neighbour twists in his seat. "Eh, Pano, shut up. We don't want that sort of talk, especially not to a foreigner."

This is enough to start a vociferous argument between them, and I'm free to gaze out of the window at the view.

We're descending sharply and the view has suddenly opened up. A vast arena extends the far side of a broad, steeply-sided and winding valley. On our side, the land bulks up ahead and to the right of us, hiding what I guess is the gorge. I wonder how the hikers got on yesterday. Somewhere up there in the many creases and crevices below the peaks on the skyline lies Glikopigi where I may find them later.

Now we have reached the lowest point. A peacock blue river runs along beside the road, overhung by plane trees. There's a bridge ahead. Can this be the bridge which was blown up in 1943 by my father? It looks modern enough to date from a rebuild at that time. We're across and climbing in a series of sharp turns on the other side. I don't like to look out of the window as the ground falls away steeply. The back of the bus projects over nothing at each corner. I wish I'd chosen a seat nearer the front.

My neighbour is pointing something out. "Before the road was built in the 1970s, there was just a cobbled path with lots of steps. We came and went by mule."

"Or on our own two feet," puts in another passenger.

From what they say, I understand that this is not my father's bridge. There'd be no reason to blow up this link to a tiny mountain village. The bridge I want is definitely on an asphalted road, a strategic traffic link between Yannina and a further town. It must lie further downstream where the river enters the plain. Feeling excited but apprehensive as well, I know I'll find the place my father fell very soon. It has become not so much a place as the man himself – Alex.

Later the same day

At last I've arrived. He must have known this village, walked its alleyways between high, grey-stone walls. The thought gives me a strange feeling, hard to identify. It's as though he's lurking, waiting for me, just around the next corner, while I know very well that he's not. Would I recognise him, even if he were? Sometimes I picture him as the attractive, young man leaning on the Colebrook orchard gate, looking towards the camera, that is, towards Joan, not me, with a half-smile. Other times, I see him in uniform, but this is a fuzzy image built up from photographs in a book about the Special Operations Executive. I've brought this book with me, hoping to find Alex in its pages – or, more realistically, some clues as to the context of his life and death. But I've never been a great reader. I like my information given to me 'live', not reported on a page. I've had this SOE book for over a year, and it's still unread. Now it's been joined on my bedside table by *Hidden Gold*. I'm more likely to manage this last one: it has only 50 pages. And its subject matter could be extremely interesting to me. It's about the sovereigns that were dropped for the groups of resistance fighters, or so I've gathered from a glance at the introduction.

The room I'm in is austere. A deep, concrete ledge links two halves of a platform on which there are rug-covered mattresses, a double and a single. There's a fireplace and chimney breast in the centre, but no sign of a fire being lit. There are radiators for the winter. I've been given a room for three people which seems over-generous. On the other hand, I think all the rooms in the guesthouse are designed in this manner. Traditional architecture, says Michalakis, the owner, who is a cousin of the woman on yesterday's bus who handed me his card, and his hotel is the very one that Rachel booked me into. This would be a greater coincidence if there were more than three places to stay in the village. Holly's hostel is one of the three. I'm going to meet her later today. Her text came through on my mobile a moment ago. *Hi Gran got here find me this pm xo H*

As I read, I can hear her voice, breathy and rushed, coming out of a mouth shaped in the same arc as Rachel's and mine, upper lip protruding slightly over the lower. (*Duck's beak*, the twins used to chant before I escaped to boarding school). I hadn't fully appreciated our family likeness until I saw a selfie of the three us, which Holly took during our spa afternoon at an Exeter hotel. The treat was Rachel's present to each of us, promised at the time of our April birthdays. The photo shows us in white towelling bathrobes, smiling up at the camera in much the same way but the faces around those smiles – how sadly different! The photo looks like an advertisement for dentistry, celebrating its progress through the decades. My 1940 teeth, uneven and yellowed; Rachel's 1960s teeth, white and well-shaped; and in the middle Holly's 1990s set – brilliantly white and perfectly even. Ah well. We cannot change the time of our birth. At least none of my teeth are false. I can chew tough meat.

II CHAPTER FIVE

Yes, I can still chew and this is a particularly chewy piece of old sheep that Michalakis has served up. Holly, being vegan, is doing better with her *horiatitki*, the country salad nowadays known in English as a Greek salad. I'm utterly content to be sitting here opposite her – she's so lovely to look at, with her bright eyes, glowing skin and natural grace. I've quite got used to all the piercings, even the row of silver studs up the rim of her right ear.

"So what was *your* journey like?" she asks me now, having told me about all the hiccups on her own.

"Well," I begin and hesitate. The mutton's chewiness gives me a good reason to pause. Whose fault was it, I ask myself, that I ended up in the wrong village? Rachel's or Holly's? I should have looked after my own arrangements, I know. But they like to help. In a way, it suits us all if I appear more incapable than I am. How could I have run the rural sales department of Halberts for so many years if I wasn't super-organised. But we don't mention that. "Well," I begin again, having swallowed with difficulty the last lump of meat, "it all went very smoothly. I liked the stretches on the various buses. And I did get to see Tesserahori on my way here, which was excellent."

"On your way here?"

"It's on the other side of the mountain." I remember now that it was Holly who made the muddle, suggesting that Glikopigi was part of Tesserahori, the reason why I got on the wrong bus. Sometimes I wonder how she managed to get into university, she goes around in such a fog. She's very young, of course, and I probably inhabited the same hazy corner of the universe at her age.

She's asking me if that was where my father was in the war.

"No. At least, I don't think so. I've got masses to find out, if I can." Even if she hasn't retained the details, I appreciate the way Holly is interested in my hunt; far more so than Rachel who'd prefer me to be at home, ready to help out with her Irish wolfhounds which she should never have taken on in her busy life. "Tell me about your group. When do you start? Where's the site?"

Holly fills me in, first by describing the people she's with in a low voice. Four of them are eating at a nearby table. There's Paul, the one with sandy-coloured hair and dark glasses with jazzy frames. He's the leader and it's his second year on this dig. He's half-Greek and has some kind of connection with the village. The colour that touches Holly's cheekbones, as she gives me this background, makes me think he could be the sole reason she's here. Vicky is the girl on his right, waving her arms about as she talks. The other two – Holly hasn't learnt their names, or can't remember them – are an item, she says. She doesn't think they'll be much help with the excavation; too obsessed with each other. This leads me to ask about Nigel, her own partner. Rachel and I worry that she treats him badly; we call him Poor Niggle. Apparently, he's gone to New York for the whole summer, so maybe not Poor Niggle after all.

"And whereabouts is the dig?"

She tells me it's an hour's walk from the village. "And it's not really a dig, Paul says. It's more of a shovel."

I smile. "A shovel!"

"We're going to be combing the earth on the floor of a cave for ancient animal bones." She finishes her salad, eating and talking at the same time – something frowned on in my youth. She describes the people who used the cave, Paleolithic hunters who herded wild animals into the gorge to pick off the weak ones with rocks, to slaughter and butcher. "The original Flintstones," she says. "Come and find us one day."

"I don't want to get in your way."

"Oh, Paul won't mind. It's all very relaxed."

When we finish our meal, she leads me over to meet him and the others. Even the couple who are in love take the time to look up and smile. Paul half-stands to shake my hand. Nice young people, I think. I promise to visit the cave one day; then I leave them for my room. I'm ready for *Hidden Gold*.

I get to page three with mounting interest and then a name jumps out at me. *Captain Alex Pritchard.* I feel exclamation marks streaming through me. I'm inclined to text Holly at once but restrain myself. I will learn more first.

The writer of the book, a New Zealander called Leonard, known by his mates as Lenny, was with Alex in the Special Operations Executive, first in France, then in northern Greece. Lenny was Alex's radio operator.

My hands are trembling so much I can barely read the dancing text.

They were sent to Cairo to be briefed before being dropped in the Pindos mountains. Leonard describes how he realised that something had gone badly wrong for Alex. He'd been the last to jump. Although Lenny and the reception committee of resistance fighters searched for a long time, there was no sign of Alex on the landing ground, a plateau high in the mountains. They gathered up the dropped supplies and cleared the area of parachutes but they had to leave before dawn. The Sarakatsan shepherds who spend summers on the plateau were not to be trusted. Lenny was led to the nearest village, Ano Kipseli, one of four villages known collectively as Tesserahori. Three or more weeks went past before Lenny and Alex met up again.

My burning questions are of course centred on my father. What had happened to Alex? What was he doing during that time? I flip through the pages quickly to find out, but Lenny is more interested in describing the time he spent in Ano Kipseli. He fell in love with the daughter of the group's leader, a Kapetan Achilles, and returned after the war to find and marry her. This is the romantic story behind the 'Londoner' who had rebuilt a ruin in the 1980s, as related to me in the Ano Kipseli taverna. As for the gold, Lenny spent several summers with a metal detector, trawling the plateau for sovereigns. The villagers were certain that supplies had been buried in different places on the mountain during the war years. Whether anything was ever found, no-one let on.

I've only skimmed the fifty pages but I've got the basic story. There is an epilogue, written by Lenny's son William, who's probably about my age. He adds that Captain Alex Pritchard lost his life during the mission to blow up the bridge at the mouth of the gorge. Lenny remained to work with the replacement officer for the rest of the occupation.

It's puzzling that Lenny didn't write about the act of sabotage and Alex's death. He does come across as self-absorbed so he may just have wanted to concentrate on his own story. Or perhaps he assumed all the details of the operation and the loss of Captain Alex had been covered in official documents – the kind of bald information contained in documents I might find in the Imperial War Museum. I prefer conversations on the spot. I've only been at it a day and already I've learnt a lot.

In the morning, I will ask Michalakis the way to the high mountain plateau. I must see the place where my father landed. I also want to meet the Sarakatsan shepherds who, according to Lenny's account, were (and maybe still are?) "not to be trusted". I recall my conversation on the bus from Igoumenitsa to Yannina and the black-clad widow who gave me Michalakis's card. He and she are cousins, members of a Sarakatsan family. So is Michalakis not to be trusted? Or did Lenny and his informants succumb to the way we divide people into Them and Us, the Them always falling short of our own standards. I should make up my own mind.

Next day
The best way to tackle a long and steep climb is to think hard of something entirely different. This is the trick I learnt on Dartmoor.

But Dartmoor tors are pimples compared to this mountain. I've been head down, putting one foot in front of the other, slowly, determinedly, for a long hour or more. The mountainside feels like a wall reaching to the sky. I'm hot and tired and I have not been left to my thoughts. I have a talkative companion who is much the same age as I am but male and fit. He could bound up this mountain in no time at all but he's kindly keeping to my pace. I'm not sure whether I'm pleased or cross about this. He's called Heinrich and he comes from Munich. I find him disturbing. He is tall and has rather well-shaped legs which emerge from shorts. Most, but not all, of his wild head of greying hair is tied in a pony tail and threaded through the back elastic of a baseball cap. Side wings hang around his face and merge with his beard. He could stride onto a stage and sing Wagner – he'd be an elderly, dark Wotan rather than young, blond Siegfried. He's staying at Michalakis's place, too, and it was Michalakis who suggested we visit his Sarakatsan shepherd relations together.

Heinrich and I met over the jug of orange juice at breakfast. He speaks Greek as well as he speaks English. He is a lecturer at Ludwig Maximilian University and an authority on the flora and fauna of the Pindos mountains. This is his third visit to Glikopigi.

"Is the best base to access the gorge," he says, "which has wonderful examples of the more rare plants."

He gives me nuggets of information at each bend in the zigzag path.

"You have heard of the Glikopigi Doctors? No? People came from far away to be treated by them."

We trudge on.

"The last of the doctors was a young Romanian girl who was known for her remedies. Sadly, she fell."

"Fell?"

"Yes. From high up in the gorge. She was after a plant which I think might have been Carduus marianus." He gives me a quick sidelong glance and lets me have the common name. "Milk thistle. Good for lactating mothers. She slipped. Five hundred metres. They found her next day. She left a child, not much more than a baby. Her sister took care of it."

"How sad."

At the next bend, Heinrich goes on. "The sister is still alive. A very old lady but in complete possession of her mental capacities."

I stop. A very old lady might have known my father! "Where does she live? In Glikopigi?"

"Not all the time. She comes and goes from Yannina."

"But you've met her?"

"Yes, but she doesn't know anything about plants."

Heinrich is back to plants.

I'm pretty well done for when we reach our first target, a cairn of stones on a ridge. "I'm going to sit and rest for a while," I tell Heinrich.

"Of course."

"You can go on."

"No, I will stay with you."

We drink from our water bottles and eat the oranges Michalakis gave us. I gaze at the view with greater appreciation now that I can breathe more normally. The ridge on which we're sitting links two peaks. Below is what Leonard of *Hidden Gold* called the plateau. I see it is an undulating, grassy plain, ringed by other peaks. It doesn't look at all suitable as a landing ground for parachutists. Directly below us is a circle of water reflecting the blue of the sky. I can see a few sheep and a collection of grey stone huts. Looking back the way we came, there is no sign of the village but I can tell where it must lie. The line of the gorge further below is clear. It's as though the mass of mountain has been riven in two jagged halves by a giant's chainsaw. I can just make out a gleam of asphalt road circling a tree-covered hilltop. Beyond, further ranges recede in bands of violet-grey, fading to the far horizon. Albania.

"You see the lake?" Heinrich is pointing.

"Yes." More pond than lake.

"It is the habitat of a newt of the salamander order. Mesotriton alpestris. But nowadays it is known as Ichthyosaura alpestris." He glances at me and adds with a smile, "Alpine newt."

I'm beginning to like him. "What I'd *really* like to know," I tell him, "is the name of the old lady. The sister of the plant collector?"

He thinks for a minute. "It's something like Eleni. Eliane. No, that's not it. Give me a moment .Ah yes. *Ileana.*"

I file the name carefully in my memory. I will find Ileana.

Heinrich has become curious about me and asks a few leading questions. We establish that we have both lost partners in the last two years.

"It's beneficial," he says, "to take a holiday, not at once, but this year I have been ready. You too?"

"Yes."

"What made you choose this area? You like mountains? Wildlife?" He's already guessed that neither are at all likely motivations for my being here. How shall I answer? He'd understand, I'm sure; he seems a sympathetic person even if he talks like the translation of a text book. I'm on the brink of telling him my purpose. *I want to find the place where my father was shot by the Germans.* No, I can't say that!

Instead I say, "We loved Greece, Richard and I. Being here brings him close." That's true.

"Yes. I know. It hurts but a healing hurt? Bitter medicine?"

He's right.

"Actually," I've begun before I can stop myself, "I'm here to find the place my father was killed in the war."

Heinrich stops and turns. "Ach, that is a very sad reason."

I was right to tell him. Of course this present-day German is not responsible for my father's death. The logical part of my brain knows that perfectly well. It's the emotional part that gets in the way.

"He was parachuted in from Cairo. He landed somewhere on this plain. I want to find and talk to one of the shepherds who might know something about it."

We continue down and onto the plain. As we approach the lake, there's an outbreak of barking a distance away. A number of dogs – four, five, no, six - are racing towards us. I'm not too happy about this and hang back behind Heinrich. When the dogs – large, scruffy, greyish-white beasts– are within twenty yards or so, they slow down to form a ferociously barking line, swinging their heads, waving their tails. They look as though they are urging each other forward to attack. Heinrich knows what to do. He bends as though to pick up a stone and the dogs back away. He moves towards them, picking up another imaginary stone. The dogs turn tail.

"Fantastic!"

Heinrich looks pleased. "I am never certain the trick will work. But it does every time."

"Thank heavens."

Still, we are both relieved when a shepherd appears from a hut and takes command of the animals. He is Michalakis's cousin and soon we are sitting on a wooden bench outside his hut, drinking *tsipouro*.

I realise that it is a good thing that Heinrich is with me. For one thing, his Greek is fluent. For another, I don't think Socrates – yes, that is his name! – would have talked to me, were I on my own. He's a contained, stern and upright old man who has taken ages to get to the point of talking at any length. Heinrich has been patient, gently gaining his trust. He first of all explained the reason for my presence. Socrates regarded me with small, bright eyes below overhanging eyebrows. I must have passed the test because he's begun to talk. This is what I've learnt so far. Socrates was a ten-year-old at the time of the landing in which one parachutist overshot the plateau and disappeared down the big ravine that leads sharply down into the gorge. He was the only one to notice this. Members of his and the other Sarakatsan families were competing to whisk away as many containers as they could before the *andartes* reached them.

"We are honourable people. We deserved to be helped by the British. We don't take sides, not against the Germans, not against the communists, not against the monarchists. It was the same in the days of the Ottomans. We travel freely, minding our own business, not making trouble. We harm no-one. No-one harms us. How else could we live our life, tending our flocks, travelling great distances twice a year, from the plains to the mountains and back again, the Sarakatsan pattern of life here in Greece and in all the countries that were under the Ottoman yoke and, before those five hundred years, from time immemorial?"

Now he's begun to talk, he speaks slowly and clearly and with solemn pride. I follow easily.

"The day after that landing I crossed the plateau and started down the ravine. I didn't know what to expect. A dead man? A wounded man? Or no-one at all. For a ten year old, you can imagine, this was a big adventure. First I found, near the top of the ravine, a container. I knew the sort that contained gold and which contained boots or clothes, rice and flour. This one would have contained gold. But it was too heavy to lift on my own, so I left it there and continued down the gully. It's full of big boulders and steep drops. The best way down is not in the bed of the ravine but higher, through the trees that grow up its sides. You have to know the way. To find the soldier, I had to stay in the watercourse. I clambered down, slipping from one level to another and, about one third of the way down to the gorge, I found the poor soul. He looked dead but in fact he was breathing. I stared at him a long time, trying to decide what to do."

Socrates goes silent as he picks up the bottle of tsipouro and fills his and Heinrich's glass. I'd like some more but say nothing. Heinrich notices and indicates my glass. Socrates raises his eyebrows, looks disapproving but relents. I get a refill. I need it. I'm riveted by this story. Here I am, sitting on the mountain plateau where my father was dropped. I am close to the ravine where he landed, hurt from the fall! Looking dead! *Please go on, Socrates.* He does.

"Your health," he says. We all clink the tiny glasses of spirit.

"And then -?" prompts Heinrich.

"And then I left him. I climbed back up through the trees. It's impossible to climb up the watercourse. That's why I knew he'd gone on down into the gorge when I returned and found him gone. It was a relief. I'd taken some days to return and dreaded finding him dead. I never told anyone. There never was a good moment. I should have said something at once, but I didn't."

"May I ask why not?" That's Heinrich. Whatever I ask, Socrates pays no attention.

"Because I wanted to keep the knowledge of the container of sovereigns to myself. There! That's honest. This is the first time I have spoken of it. I do so in honour of *Kiria* Eleni."

Mrs Eleni. I like that.

"She's come all this way to discover what happened to her father."

"And did you ever hear what happened to him - that is, after he got out of the ravine?"

"No. But we learnt of the destruction of the road bridge by the *andartes* a month or two later. He must have had something to do with it."

"Yes, he did! He blew up the bridge! He was killed by the Germans but he'd succeeded!" In my excitement, I've spoken without thought of Heinrich's feelings. We used to be enemies.

II CHAPTER SIX

I'm dawdling over my second cup of coffee, watching other people's busy-ness. There's a Monday morning feeling even in this holiday setting. Holly and her group have gone off to start work in the cave. The other foreigners staying here have asked their questions of Michalakis and his Albanian wife Maria and have gone their separate ways. Maria has cleared the breakfast tables and taken delivery of quantities of potatoes. This morning she's wearing sparkling gold ballet shoes and white tights under a short flowery tunic, an extraordinary ensemble. I admire her self-confidence and wish I could describe the scene for Richard. He would have revelled in it.

Now here comes Heinrich. He's wished me good morning and is about to leave. He is going to drive down to the river and walk upstream to its source. He says water held in the icy limestone heart of the mountain collects within it, sinks to the gorge floor and then rises to form pools that become the river almost at once.

"Like the parting of the Red Sea by Moses." He stands with two hands on the back of the chair opposite mine. He won't sit down. "Water on one side, dry riverbed on the other."

I'd like to go with him but he's not offering to take me. Pay-back time? He must have thought yesterday that I was laying the blame for my father's death at his door. I don't see how I can retrieve the situation without making it worse.

A familiar feeling comes over me. In my inner centre there's a bottomless, unfillable void. Regret is a feeble word for it but it is regret for things that never were - or once were and can never be again.

"Have a good time," I tell him.

"And you? What is your plan for the day?"

Yes, I must get together a plan for the day. A plan to stuff into the mouth of the void. Right at this moment, I cannot think what it will be, but I'm answering.

"Exploration," I say. "Generally ...exploring. Round and about."

From the terrace of the taverna the hairpin bends of the road descending to the river are intermittently visible. I watch out for the green car which I know belongs to Heinrich. A hired Nissan. I'm car-less. Does he know that?

"Did you find my cousin? Socrates?" Michalakis is at my elbow with a jug of coffee and a spare cup in his hands.

The void will be filled. "Yes! I did! And yes, I'd love more coffee! Please join me, if you have the time."

He obviously does have the time. He's more than ready to sit and chat. He obviously knew – before asking - that I found Socrates. He knows, too, why I'm here, although he makes a pretence of not knowing. Socrates would have reached for his phone before Heinrich and I had gone a hundred yards. Shepherds living in huts on remote mountains were probably the first users of mobiles.

I recapture the excitement I experienced yesterday, my sadness gone in an instant. I tell Michalakis what I'd learnt. "It's fantastic! He actually *saw* my father!"

"That's good. Now you will have to talk to Yiannis. He is the same age as Socrates."

He tells me that Yiannis was a member of the *andartes* who operated in the area. "Would you like me to phone him?"

Is this getting too easy? I hardly dare believe how close I am. Someone who was with my father, who could have reached out a hand and touched him, is here, now, alive. I'm a living hand away from touching my father myself.

My heart is thumping as I reach Yiannis's house, and not just because of the steep incline. I pause to catch my breath and calm down before knocking on the double wooden door set in the high stone wall. *Yiannis will be expecting you*, Michalakis told me. *Just go on in.*

It doesn't seem right to barge in. I'm familiar enough with the local architecture from the postcards I've seen in the taverna and from mugging up on the internet before arrival. These lych gates in high stone walls, which I've passed at intervals on my way up through the village, open onto courtyards. Each house sits within its own courtyard. I know that if the householder is out, he threads a stick through the brass rings on the twin doors. No stick means he's at home and you can just go in, calling out his name. Or hers, as the case may be.

There's no stick balanced between the rings. Yiannis is at home. I compromise and give a knock while calling out as I enter. Will he be deaf? How old must he be? If he was a member of the *andartes* group, then he's older than Socrates who was 10 in 1943.

There are two buildings within the courtyard, one much smaller than the other. It has just one storey. It has a door with a fly-screen over a half-window. Shall I knock on this door? Or the more imposing front door of the bigger, two-storey house? I hesitate.

"Haaa!" The loud, sudden exclamation startles me.

Yiannis has appeared from yet another building, one that links the other two, and is coming towards me with arms flung out. Words are being flung out, too – a stream of greeting that's impossible to take in but includes my name and my father's repeatedly. I feel for a dizzily strange instant that I've been here before, done this before, been greeted like this before.

I'm hugged, then pushed back for examination, then pulled into his embrace again. Yiannis can't get over that he's looking at the daughter of Kapetan Aleko! It can't be true! He laughs continually, flashing a row of teeth revealing a gleam of gold in each corner of his mouth. Aleko's daughter! Here! In Glikopigi! Let me look at you! Yes! I see it! You have his mouth, his eyes! Come in, come in.

Yiannis is in the middle of repairing his roof. I'm to forgive the pile of stones and the dust. (I hadn't noticed either until he mentioned them). He leads me through the fly-screened door into a kitchen. There's a woman sitting at a table in the corner of the room. She is holding her head, her elbows on the table. She doesn't look up. There's no need for Yiannis to explain. I've guessed from her manner – I know the signs - she has dementia. *That puts paid to any hope of memories coming from her.* I'm ashamed by my immediate, selfish thought.

But there's nothing wrong with Yiannis's memory. He's telling me about his first meeting with Aleko, talking non-stop as he brews up coffee on a camping gas stove. I've already had two large cups of instant, but I can't refuse.

"Sit down, sit down. Don't pay attention to Poppy, the poor thing. She's alright."

I sit down beside her. She moves a hand from her head slowly and lays it, palm down, on the table between us. She doesn't look up. It's an automatic gesture, left over – I guess - from the time when she was in control, welcoming visitors to her kitchen. I cover her hand with mine and we sit like that until Yiannis brings the coffee to the table and two glasses of cold water. I wonder if Poppy ever met Aleko.

"I hope you like it medium? I'm such a fool, I forgot to ask."

Yiannis has a high-pitched giggle which erupts every so often, as though he's being tickled. His ebullience is infectious. It sounds as though he had a wonderful time in the war. He gives me the picture of a young lad roaming freely and without fear over the mountainous landscape, hunting chamois, hares, wild boar, dragging back anything he managed to shoot to the cave for the men to roast over a fire. Fish in the river, too, trout as big as *this* – demonstrating with his hands spread wide.

"Cave? What cave? Where?" He hears my questions eventually.

"The cave where Pavlos comes with his students."

Holly's cave! It must be. Pavlos is Paul.

"Archaeology students?"

"Yes. He brings a group each year. A clever boy he is. Man, I suppose, now. University in England."

Yiannis now goes off on another line of thought, talking about his own children and grandchildren. All the young people of the village grow up and leave for cities. "If you'd come here ten, twenty years ago, you'd have seen a sad village, abandoned houses, roofs collapsed. Once water gets in ... I keep on repairing mine. All very well to put conservation orders on old buildings, but when you have to live in them, look after them ... it's a never-ending job."

He says this cheerfully. I have the impression that he's happy to have household jobs to do, even if he is an old man. I reckon he must be around 90.

"Coffee alright?"

I nod. But it's the glass of cold water that I appreciate. I wonder how I can get him back to 1943. At the next pause when Yiannis syphons up a large mouthful of coffee, I tell him that I met Socrates yesterday – "up on the mountain where my father landed."

Yiannis looks at me over the rim of the gold-rimmed coffee cup. "Yes, I know."

"Were you there?"

"Yesterday. No." The evasion is a tease. There's a gleam of gold in his smile.

"No, I mean, in the war, when my father and the wireless operator were dropped by plane. Were you there then?"

He looks at me and then away. I have the feeling that he's turning over many memories in his mind to select what he wants to tell me – and what he does not.

"I met them later. When we were living in the cave. I spent a lot of time watching Lenny, the wireless operator. He was the reason why I made a career in telecommunications."

He goes on about his life as a government employee. "Early retirement in those days too! And a decent pension. I've been retired far longer than I ever worked."

I try to get him back to the war years. "Socrates – " I begin.

"Socrates, yes. Good for him," he says. "He's carrying on the old way of life. But as for the rest ---the sons don't follow the fathers. Who wants to be a shepherd these days, when there's money to be made from tourism. The Sarakatsan, like Michalakis, are building big hotels."

I've lost the opportunity. Yiannis is now talking of the difference between the traditional inhabitants of the village and the shepherd families. In the past, the Sarakatsan never owned houses; they might rent in the summer months, for the benefit of their wives and children, and for ease of handling the produce, the milk, meat and cheese-making, while the men looked after the sheep on the mountains, but in the autumn all the families would depart with the flocks to spend the winter on the plains as far away as Igoumenitsa.

"This morning I saw a flock of goats being herded out of the village onto the mountainside. Do they belong to a Sarakatsan family?"

"Oh no! The villagers are the ones who have goats." Yiannis makes it sound as though I've made a gross social misjudgement. This is the flavour of his conversation. *We* have goats and own the houses. *They* are sheep-herders, mountain dwellers, only here half a year. Hence, the idea that they cannot be trusted?

Soon I get up to leave because Yiannis wants to get on with his roof-mending. I make a kind of bowing gesture towards Poppy. Her head is back in her hands but now she looks up and beckons me close with a single crooked finger. I lean down to hear her whisper.

It's hard to make out what she says exactly but I understand she wants me to ask or maybe tell someone something. I bend closer and take hold of her hand. She nods her head vigorously and whispers. I register names. "Aleko... Telis's house ... find Nikos."

"Poppy!" Yiannis's voice is sharp. "They're dead! Telis and Nikos are dead!" Then he turns to me. "Don't pay attention. She's out of her mind."

I go back to the guesthouse feeling shaken. The way Poppy looked at me made me feel she saw my father.

II CHAPTER SEVEN

Joan's friend Sheena has Alzheimer's. It's been developing over the last three years. Joan says it's like losing a friend by slow degrees. That's what makes it so particularly painful. I try to visit Joan more often these days, because she has lost so many friends. "What else can I expect," she says when I commiserate. "I've lived far too long. People of my age should be put down."

She says this as a kind of joke, but she's serious, too. It's hard to hear.

I usually respond by saying, "Well, I'm selfish. I want you to stick around for many more years."

I dread losing her, but I do understand her attitude. I'll be the same. We are alike. We never got on very well when I was growing up, becoming more and more my own person. Independent, stubborn, private – just like her. I felt ousted by the twins, and even more so when I was sent away to school and they never were. I developed protective coating. I took on the grumpy, childish attitude summed up by the unspoken message: *if you don't want me, I will not want you* before *you don't want me.*

"I did my best for you," says Joan.

Whose "best" though?

Who knows what's best for anyone?

Heinrich is approaching the table where I'm drinking a beer. I can feel myself slipping at once into that childish frame of mind. *As you didn't want me to join you today, I shall ignore you.*

I tell myself sternly to grow up.

"Heinrich! Come and join me!"

"I was on my way." He pulls out a chair and sits down. "Would you like another?" He is twisting to catch the eye of Maria who is flitting hither and thither on her golden slippers. "How was your day?"

I can never maintain resentment for very long. I do not have the courage of my convictions, mainly because I have no convictions to be courageous about. I'm a weathervane turning with the wind, from whatever quarter it blows. I envy the people who know what they think and stick with it. Yet this may not always be an enviable characteristic. I think of Yiannis and his prejudices against the Sarakatsan: how they cannot be trusted. Lenny in his book said the same thing. I think this is more likely a reflection of the speakers' own untrustworthiness rather than that of others. I must remember this whenever I listen eagerly to information about the war years.

"Fruitful," I tell Heinrich. "At least, it seemed so at the time. I met someone who was a young lad in '43. He was a member of the resistance group my father led."

"Good God! That's a great connection."

"I thought so, too. But I'm not so sure. He was forthcoming to begin with. Then he wanted to change the subject."

"Not unexpected? They were difficult years."

There's a momentary silence between us. I shall be brave. "Heinrich – you and I – we can talk about the war, can't we? We weren't responsible."

"Of course we can." He smiles at me across the table. The golden ballet shoes are dancing closer. Heinrich manages to catch Maria's eye and orders more beer and another glass. Then he leans towards me and says with a lowered voice, "I was a boy in Dresden."

I am aghast.

"Everyone suffered at the time, in one way or another, wherever they were," he says.

I think back to my one year of war babyhood followed by a childhood growing up on a farm in Devon. Sweets were rationed but that was not a hardship. You don't miss what you never had. Joan did talk of the bombing of Exeter, but that happened before I was born. My first memories were all of dreamy, hazy nature, endless sunny afternoons, daffodils bending their heads in a breeze against a deeply blue sky, the smell of roses, newly laid eggs, brown-shelled and warm in the palm of my hand.

Heinrich is holding his glass of beer towards me. "We will drink to the century we are now in and be glad that we haven't fought each other for sixty and more years!"

"To Peace, long it may it reign."

"I once thought, if ever I had a child, a daughter, I would call her Irene."

"Peace - a lovely name. But you didn't?"

"No, all boys. Four of them!"

And now we are onto families.

We decide to eat at another taverna which Heinrich thinks is good. "Chicken on the *skara*. Or chops, if you prefer." We can smell the meat dripping juice onto the burning charcoal before we've even entered. I realise I'm hungry in a way I haven't been for a very long time.

Breakfasttime and no-one is around. How extraordinary to have let my granddaughter slip out of my mind! I realise I didn't see her at all yesterday, and now she and the group will have left for the cave an hour or more ago. Still, this is as it should be. I didn't come here to be a bothersome old granny.

In a day or two I'll suggest to Heinrich that we find the cave together. I'll ask the group leader – Paul? – and Holly first of course.

Today, we're going to drive to Tesserahori. I'm finding him easy, and welcome, company. This surprises me. I haven't been expecting to make any new friends since I lost Richard. I must be coming out of the first stages of bereavement, as designated in all the self-help books. What stage am I into now? Re-socialisation? New friending? I'll say this to Heinrich - it seems we are at much the same point in our grieving. There are times we need to be alone; times we need company. Yesterday over our meal he told me that he needed to be alone. His honesty washed away the grumpy child who was going to be hurtful before being hurt.

I know I'll never experience again the precious feeling of safe familiarity that a long relationship provides, an everyday feeling taken for granted until it's lost. But that shouldn't stop me for welcoming whatever, whoever, may come into the void. It may not be Heinrich – it's ridiculous to think it might be, when we've only just met – yet there is something about him that makes me entertain the idea ...well, I shan't say more. I don't want to jinx whatever may come in the future.

He's approaching right now.

He stands to attention beside the table, clicks his heels and raises a hand to his forehead. "Gut morgen, Frau Eleni." It's a military salute, not a Heil Hitler. Is he teasing me? Challenging me? I smile up at him uneasily.

Ano Kipseli

Matheos of the taverna greets me like a long-lost relation. "Kiria Eleni!" I'm clasped in his arms and kissed on both cheeks. I suspect his warmth doesn't go deep. Or maybe he's mistaking me for another foreigner, one he knows better.

"And Kirios Enrico! Excellent."

Apparently Heinrich spent some time staying here so he could explore the higher end of the gorge. Now he's discussing with Matheos what we can eat for lunch. I decide on a plate of mountain greens and a fried egg. Heinrich will have bean soup.

I get *Hidden Gold* out of my shoulderbag. "I musn't forget to return this." I put it on the table Matheos is getting ready for us.

"You finished it?"

"It's not long."

"You know the book, Enrico? By our local writer?"

Heinrich hasn't read the book but I've told him about Lenny. He heard, too, the story of the botched landing as related by the Sarakatsan shepherd. While I'm on the hunt for links to my father, Heinrich is keen to find out if the canister of gold sovereigns that Socrates saw as a boy was ever found. He's convinced it could still be lying at the top of the big ravine. While we wait for Matheos to prepare our meal, Heinrich talks about gold and its value. Sovereigns are being used as currency nowadays, he says. The disastrous state of Greece's economy is the reason why.

"The Greeks went mad when they entered the common market. The Olympics was another disaster. They borrowed money to the hilt, and no-one wants to pay taxes."

"Who does."

"True. But here they are experts at not paying. That's on the level of the individual citizen. Nationally, they have a debt of enormous proportions to the European Community. The interest payments are beyond their capability. They may have to - what is it called in English?"

He thinks of the word before I come up with a suggestion.

"Default, yes. Sovereigns have become the only safe currency. In Athens they're queuing at the central bank to buy them at a price that goes up daily. I hear a single sovereign can cost over 270 euros!"

I can suddenly see the attraction of finding a canister full of gold sovereigns. But what would the rights and wrongs of that be? Who would own it? The British government or the remnants of the resistance group? Or finder's keepers?

Heinrich has continued to talk. "It must still be there," he says in conclusion.

"It couldn't possibly be after all those years," I say firmly. "Socrates must have returned to the ravine to look for it. Other shepherds, too, would have come across it. They wouldn't leave it just lying there."

"Ah, but I know how impossible it is to follow the dry watercourse from the top of the ravine. It's a jumble of big rocks and sheer drops from one level to the next. I know, because I've tried it when I've been looking for plants. I believe that the gold is still there, waiting for us to find it!"

"Well, Lenny's son tried. He wrote an Epilogue to the book. Here, read it!"

"I don't need to read it. I will find the gold."

We turn our attention to our food.

Later

Hoping to learn something useful to help us on our separate hunts, we've followed Matheos's directions to Mikro Kipseli to find the house of Lenny's son. He told us Oooeeleeam should be there. This is the way the name is pronounced in a language without a W in its alphabet. Richard and I had a friend called William who came with us when we were sailing around the Cyclades.

William, according to Matheos, will be expecting us. Of course he will. News buzzes quickly from one mobile to another

We left the car in Ano Kipseli, in the parking space gouged out of the mountain where the bus arrives and departs, and where I arrived and departed just a few days ago. It feels like a month. Although it might have been easier to walk down the asphalt road, we preferred to follow the old cobbled paths that lead down through each village linking all four. Mikro Kipseli is the first of the four. It lies the far side of a beautiful old arched bridge, and its few houses huddle together on the hillside, grey on grey, surrounded by the dark green of trees and shrubs. Holm oak, says Heinrich, and juniper.

Heinrich asks me to pose halfway over the bridge with the village behind me. I agree, ungraciously. I loathe having a camera pointed at me, even if it is only the small lens on the back of a mobile phone. I wonder if I might take a similar photo of Heinrich, but dismiss the thought as soon I imagine Rachel receiving it. "*Mum ...!*" She'd be horrified to see my new companion – *any* new companion, but a pony-tailed one! Sometimes I feel that Rachel is my mother, not my daughter.

Heinrich puts away his phone, then raises an arm as I begin to walk on. For a ludicrous second I think he's going to hug me. But it's just a gesture to make me stop and look at the view from the bridge. "You see how the land folds in? We're at the very start of the gorge. Water runs under this bridge in the wintertime."

"You've been here in the winter?"

He nods.

We go on across and into the village, past a memorial in a small square – plane tree and café essential and typical ingredients – then climb stone steps counting the numbers on the wooden doors set in the high stone walls either side of the path, each under its own sheltering roof. It isn't hard to find William and his wife Kathy. They're sitting on the balcony of a house, its upper storey visible above and behind the path wall.

"Just come right in. The door is open."

I find my estate agent's experience coming to the fore as we enter. The first impression is of perfection. Then I take in the detail. Large, wide-mouthed amphora flank the shallow steps leading into the stone paved courtyard. They hold arrangements of flowers – pink and white pelargoniums, trailing green and white ivy. In the middle of the courtyard there is triangular bed of rosemary and lavender. The two-storey house is in the shape of the letter gamma, seeming to hold the herb bed in its arms. Dark wooden shutters frame the windows. The balcony is built on top of a projecting lower part of the house. I guess this is the kitchen, remembering my visit to Yiannis yesterday. William and Kathy are on their feet, welcoming us in. William comes down steps from the balcony and shakes our hands. He looks freshly brushed and polished and smells strongly of aftershave. Kathy is behind him, white slacks, white shirt, blonde hair, a hint of blue eyeshadow and pink lipstick. I feel as though I've just emerged from a ditch. I'm conscious of Heinrich's height, muscular calves below his knee-length shorts, his pony tail. What sort of couple do we make, I wonder, in their eyes?

But of course we are not a couple and I want to make that clear.

We're now sitting on the balcony, sipping from long glasses of chilled, homemade orange juice in which float sprigs of mint. "From the garden," says Kathy with proud delight. I find myself repeating lovely, lovely to everything. It *is* lovely, all of it but in particular the view from the balcony. We're looking over the stone roofs of Mikro Kipseli to the far side of the shallow valley. The bridge we crossed is not visible but we can see the cobbled mule track that leads to it emerging from houses of the nearest village.

"Kato Kipseli," supplies Kathy. "And then it's Meso, and last of all Ano."

"Where we left the car," says Heinrich to me, as though he doubts my grasp of the layout. He does not understand how eager I am for every morsel of information I can pick up.

"Heinrich has been very kind. And we only met a couple of days ago!" There! I have made it clear. Now I'm giving them a potted account of my reason for coming to Glikopigi, and for wanting to meet them.

"Oh, we can tell you lots!" responds Kathy. "William's father came back after the war."

"That's the civil war that followed the German one," puts in William.

"And married a girl he'd met here in 1943. William's mother!"

I've certainly come to the right place. The two of them are competing to tell us as much as they can.

II CHAPTER EIGHT

I'm home again – that is, back at Michalakis's guesthouse. Strange how quickly a place becomes a home. I put my adaptability down to my boarding school life from the age of 10. Or perhaps my present feeling of home-coming is influenced by the progress in my hunt for my father. I'm drawing nearer.

This is, briefly, or not so briefly as it may develop, what I learnt today from William and Kathy. They told me Lenny's story, elaborating on the version Lenny had written himself. They took turns in a dovetailing way, each interrupting or correcting the other. They started with the landing on the plateau.

Having given up the search for Alex, Lenny and the reception committee of *andartes* went on down to Ano Kipseli. He was taken to the first house in the village and looked after by a man called Panos who was friendly and generous with the local drink.

"*Tsipouro,*" put in Kathy, taking up the tale.

Lenny was there for a few weeks, trying to work out what was happening and what he should do. He contacted Cairo, but all they said was *Wait*. He wasn't a prisoner but, if he ever went out for a wander around, he was aware of being watched. He was often invited into houses, but he felt he was on parole. There was only one house in Meso Kipseli where he could relax. The eldest daughter of the house was called Tassia, short for Anastasia.

"My mother!" said William, seizing the momentum. "Love at first sight, according to my dad. They just sat and looked at each. Neither could speak the other's language. Made no difference! They married when Lenny returned after the war."

"The civil war. But we're jumping ahead. Tell her about his friend Nikos," urged Kathy.

"Yes. Nikos's family lived in Meso Kipseli next door to Tassia's family. Lenny met him there and they became good friends. Nikos came and went between the villages. Lenny described him as a peacemaker. He thought that all the different groups of *andartes* should work together. He was a member of the group based in Glikopigi but he was also sympathetic to the local group. He brought the leader, a Kapetan Achilleas, to meet Lenny.

"Just a moment," interrupted Kathy. "Nikos always said that he joined the Glikopigi group because he was engaged to Ileana. You should find Ileana, Helen. She's still alive."

"Someone else mentioned that name to me," I put in.

"I did," said Heinrich. He was sitting close to me and patted my knee as he spoke, as though he was forgiving me a lapse of memory. Well, it was rather hopeless of me to forget what he'd told me about the plant collector. It was only yesterday. Or was it? No time to work this out as Kathy's speaking.

"Your father loved Ileana. And she, him."

William jumped in. "No! Don't say that. It gives the wrong impression."

"I meant love in the sense of liking very much."

"They were good friends. Ileana did a lot of translating between Alex and the *andartes*. That was all. She was engaged to Nikos at the time and they married. Nikos has died now but Ileana is still alive."

"I've just told her that." Kathy was indignant.

"Alright. Where were we?"

"Coming up to the battle."

"Oh yes, the battle. I don't know how much you know about the history of those years. The different groups of resistance fighters were jostling for power. The communists were looking ahead to the end of the war. They had hopes of gaining control of the government."

"Alex had been rescued from the ravine by the Glikopigi *andartes*. He'd broken his ankle. Ileana nursed him back to health. When he could walk better, he came across the mountain with the Gliko group to find Lenny."

William intervened. "Not just to find Lenny. The communist group, the ELAS, thought their rivals, the EDES based in Tesserahori, had been stealing all the supplies that should be strictly shared between them."

"Tremendous rivalry," added Kathy. "It was a raid."

"And your father found my father in Panos's house. By the way, Lenny had no idea what was going on; he was interested in Tassia, not the background politics. Whereas I've wanted to dig into the past--- in the same way as you want to."

I acknowledged this with a Greek sideways tucking in of my chin.

"Alex and Lenny went with Nikos to find Kapetan Achilleas. Their idea was to defuse the tension by setting up a meeting between the two leaders of the warring groups. They hoped to do this before the raid was due to begin. What happened next took them completely by surprise. Before they met Achilleas, Nikos led them down a back alleyway, ushered them into a warehouse and locked the door on them!"

Kathy took over. "If you ever knew my father-in-law, you'd be laughing. Lenny was brilliant at finding the funny side of things and telling funny stories. His freckly face would crease up before the punchline."

Freckles. I could now imagine Lenny as a redhead. I looked at William's greying hair and saw flecks of ginger.

"They escaped," went on William. "And then a battle broke out in another part of the village. They could hear gunfire. They decided to get the hell out and went around the back of the houses and up to the ridge. From there, they decided to get back over the mountain to Glikopigi. Lenny didn't return until after the war."

"The civil war."

"I said that the first time." Kathy smiled at William.

"That battle was like the opening salvo of the civil war."

The conversation continued as they drove us in their car back to ours. They keep their car where the road from Yannina crosses the beginnings of the gorge and climbs the mountainside in hairpin bends. It was built to skirt the houses. They pointed out the back of Tassia's family house; we were following the route that Lenny and Alex must have taken to avoid the gunfire within the villages.

"Another time," they said, "we could meet up on the mountain and go down the ravine, looking for gold!"

Heinrich liked the sound of this and asked if they still had Lenny's metal detector.

"If he didn't find the gold with that, then how will we?" I asked.

That evening

Heinrich is keen to arrange a gold-seeking day. This surprises me because he suspects Lenny of having found the gold and cashed it in. "William and Kathy are not as we say short of a pfennig." He expands on this theme over an evening drink. "How is it possible for Lenny who worked in telecommunications, to re-build a ruin in these mountains, live in central London, and holiday in New Zealand's Bay of Islands?"

Heinrich is so ready to be suspicious of Lenny, he won't be happy until he's thoroughly searched the length of the ravine. If we find no gold, he will be convinced that Lenny pocketed it all. And why, he goes on, did Lenny, whose wife was from Kipseli. call their son such an English name, so hard to pronounce in Greek?

"I smell rats," he tells me. "We will go together with William and Kathy, and I will watch them."

I am not in sympathy with his strangely antagonistic attitude. Tomorrow I'll be visiting Holly's cave and Heinrich is not going to come. Without actually saying so, we both know we need a day without each other. It feels as though we've got on too well too quickly. I look across the evening supper table at him. I can't believe I like a man who winds his grey hair through the elastic at the back of a baseball cap.

II CHAPTER NINE

There's something satisfactory about tying the laces on walking boots – at least, that's what I find. The laces criss-cross through holes from the toe cap end of the boot but as you reach the tongue, the system changes. You catch the lace around four cleats, two on each side. It makes it easier to pull the laces tight. There! How interesting life can be.

I imagine I've made Richard laugh.

It's these tiny moments of inconsequential interchange that are among the most irreplaceable.

As I stamp my way through the courtyard, Maria comes darting out of the kitchen. No gold slippers today; instead, red, strappy sandals with a wedge heel. Whenever I look at her – and I'm not usually interested in clothes, so it's unusual for me to notice what people are wearing - I think of the poverty in Albania. It's no surprise that she glories in what she can buy in Yannina. Sometimes she looks as though she's stepped out of a pantomime. In every other way, she is highly practical. The guesthouse is smoothly run, a really pleasant place to stay.

This morning she hands me a walking stick from the selection housed in a barrel for the use of visitors. She knows I'm going down to the cave by what they call the old way. I'm to look out for the chapel of Ayios Yorgos and take the side path that leads to it. After the chapel I'm to carry on down. It will be rough.

She also gives me a tin foil-wrapped package. "At least *you* will have good food." The taverna higher up the village provides midday food for the archaeologists. Rivals.

I'm off. On my own. It feels good. Down through the village, past the place where the bus turns, then I look out for the beginnings of the *kalderimi*, the stone-paved footpath that used to be the only route for people and animals from the village, down to the river and then up to join the asphalt road to Yannina. Michalakis told that it is hard to follow nowadays because sections of it were destroyed when they built the road to Glikopigi. There's talk of restoring many of the old pathways but that's all there is, says Michalakis, just talk.

It's not difficult to begin with. It looks as though a start has been made to relay the paving and re-edge the steps. I can look up from the path every now and again and take in the expansive view. After the enclosed village, it's wonderful to be alone in such a landscape under such a blue sky. A few, white trails of clouds are caught on the peaks of the mountain; which forms an amphitheatre behind me. Ahead and to my left I can see the far sides of the gorge lit by the mid-morning sun. The deeply etched cliffs look as though fingernails have been dragged down them; you can almost hear the scratching sound; better, imagine organ pipes and music. To my right, the gorge opens out and there among the dark greenery of low trees and scrubby bushes runs the invisible river. Between me and the river, somewhere on the steep hillside I'm descending lies the cave. I'm surely drawing closer to my father.

Here's Richard again, looking over my shoulder. "*Concentrate.*"

I nearly tripped on a step's kerbstone.

Still no sign of the chapel and I've been walking for nearly an hour. I never wear a watch. Heinrich, if he were with me, would be efficiently timing the walk, knowing exactly where we should be, and at what time. His voice comes into my head. He's telling me the numbers of people who lost their lives in the Dresden bombing. Yesterday evening our conversation turned to our different experiences of the second world war.

"You were just a baby in February 1945, am I right? Devon was a safe place? You had a mother, a roof over your head, food?"

I know I was lucky, I don't need to be told. But he told me.

"For three days in February 1945 my home city of Dresden was bombed. Not just by a few bombs for one or two nights. No. For three days, four thousand tons of explosives and incendiaries were dropped by American and British bombers. We went up in flames. It was a cauldron. It's a wonder any of us survived. Twenty-five thousand didn't. Civilians. Women, children, babies."

I sit there numbly. Heinrich knows the figures off pat. "I'm sorry," I mumble feebly. What else can you say?

Heinrich leans across and places his hand on mine. It momentarily reminds me of doing the same at Yiannis' house. I laid my hand on Poppy's. "We cannot be held responsible for what our country does on our behalf," he says. "Do you want to do everything Britain does and has done in the past?"

"No!"

"My family weren't Nazis. We were badly punished all the same."

I'm silent as I scrabble in my mind for something I've memorised and which I've often brought to the surface. It's dreadful the way, when I want to remember something swiftly, there's a terrible blank in my mind. The beginnings of Alzheimer's? At our age, this is what we dread. I see Poppy, her head bent over her kitchen table.

Then – I've got it! It floats to the forefront of my mind like a gift. I bring it out as neatly as Heinrich quoted figures. "'*As long as people believe in certainties, they will continue to commit atrocities.*' Voltaire!" I say triumphantly.

To my right I see something greyish-white, a building. The path is heading straight for it. The chapel. I shall go in if the door's not locked.

Inside, it's dark and smells of dust, wax, incense, mountain herbs. There is a small window high up behind the rough, wooden iconostasis. I peer behind it into the priest's den, the altar, the holy of holies. In this chapel it looks like the back scullery at Colebrook Farm, circa 1950. There's a green can of water and a handle-less broom, the usual sort that looks like a child's straw skirt gathered at the waist. The altar is a stone ledge with a grubby, embroidered cloth on it. This chapel is not being looked after as carefully as it would have been in the past. There are two icons nailed to the iconostasis: one to the Virgin Mary and one portraying St George slaying what looks more like a goat than a conventional dragon.

I shall light a candle. For the soul of my father? For the patron saint of England? For Richard? There is a cardboard box of candles and a box of matches, skewed out of shape but with a few matches left in it. There's a collection dish but with no money in it save for a coin with a hole in its centre. It's a leftover from the days of the drachma. I remember the coins from our sailing days; this coin is a *lepto*, a 100th part of a drachma. Worth a grain of sand today? I add one euro to the dish.

The rickety stand with the candle-holders is at a dangerous angle on the flag-stoned floor. There are three burnt-down stubs. I'm reassured. People do still come here. Certainly, they'll come on April 23rd, the festival of St. George, my birthday as well as Shakespeare's birth and death day. I wonder – did my father ever come here? I think it's likely. He might have been the sort of person who never passes an open door but wants to know what's inside. Ever curious, like me. I don't think he'd be religious. Joan wasn't. But I may be creating a father conveniently like me, one that I would have liked to have, not one that he would have been in reality.

As I fit my candle into a holder on the stand, I begin to feel the silence of the chapel folding around me. This is a special place. People pray here. They come and go, leaving silent prayers in the flames of the candles they light. The flame flickers and dies. The enormity of life and death and the hair's breadth between the two states floods over me. Richard died suddenly. A stroke. I had no time to say good-bye. My father died with the same lack of warning. People always say that sudden death is a blessing for the person who dies, while it makes the bereavement even more difficult.

For my father, aged only 25, death was not a blessing. For Joan, it must have been a shock but not entirely unexpected, given the war. And, as she told me several times, they hardly knew each other. Still, even if their love was brief, it may have been deeply felt and passionate, although it's hard to connect that word with Joan, the most down-to-earth person I've ever known. Pregnant with me after my father's last leave, she married Thomas soon after my birth.

So much guesswork, so many unanswered, unanswerable questions.

I turn to leave the chapel but linger a moment, wondering if it's safe to leave the candle alight. I don't want to blow it out. The flame has given the place a different atmosphere, an inhabited feeling. I have brought people in with me: Joan and Alex and Richard. People have come here over very many years to find a connection to something other than what we know to exist.

It's no surprise that humankind has always created a god or gods to take care of us in the face of the unknown. And what about rewarding the good and punishing the evil? We need someone to adjudicate. Not a fallible human being but some entity outside our world. If we didn't, we'd all be warring chimps.

But we *are* warring chimps. The image of bombed cities comes to mind. *I'm sorry*, I said to Heinrich, knowing that all the apologies in the world, given and received, for all the crimes committed by our species to one another and to our habitat, cannot re-make human history.

I close the chapel door behind me and head on down the path. It's hardly a path at all, just a narrow thread of terracotta earth and whitish-grey stones between prickly bushes and clumps of sage. The hillside descends more steeply. Then at an outcrop of rock I stop and listen. The cave must be close. Yes, voices - from somewhere below me.

"Holly?"

After calling several times, she bobs out as though from undergrowth. She points to the side of the rocky outcrop and shouts up that she thinks I might manage to get down that way.

I do, but in a very undignified slither. Stones scatter and fall below. Luckily, I don't.

"There is a much easier way," Holly tells me, as she leads me along a wide shelf of rock to meet the group. "We usually come up from the river."

They are sitting in a line outside the cave entrance, mugs in hand: Paul, Vicky, Charlie and Samantha – the last two I identify as the couple Holly described as being obsessed with each other. They make the identification easy as they are almost sitting in each other's laps. Paul hasn't got his shades on today. He looks more like an archaeologist, whatever an archaeologist is supposed to look like: khaki shorts and sleeveless jacket over a white T-shirt. The jacket has lots of button-down pockets. Safari-wear? Vicky has long, straight black hair and is very pretty.

Paul springs to his feet with outstretched hand. "Welcome to the paleolithic!"

"I don't want to get in your way."

"Don't keep saying that, Granny," whispers Holly in my ear.

"Would you like a coffee?" asks Vicky. "Or tea?"

"Just water, please."

"I'll get it, Vick," Holly ducks under the overhang of the cave and disappears inside.

"Can you manage on the ground? We don't have ---"

"Of course." I sit down next to Samantha, and cross my legs, not quite in a yoga pose but jolly nearly. I'm proud that I can.

Paul explains to me the ancient use of the cave. "It's not unlike the way of life of the present day Sarakatsani -insofar they followed a similar half-yearly shift between the plains and the mountains. The paleolithic hunters occupied the cave when the wild animals, mainly red deer, were moving from the winter shelter of the lowlands to the fresh new grass in the uplands. They'd stampede them into the gorge, create a bottleneck and stone and club the animals to death. They'd butcher them here in this cave. It would have been nearer to the river then. We are making a careful study of the bones in the earth of the cave floor to see what the animals were, the different species, numbers and so on. The cave was bigger then – in fact, it was much larger until quite recently. An earthquake in the winter of 1944 caused a rockfall in one corner of the cave. The *andartes* had been using it for storing ammunition and the stores must still be there, as well as bones in the earth from the old stone age."

An involuntary shudder passes through me. *So close.*

"We're pegging out sections and working from the front to the back, and from side to side. But it's tantalising when we get to where the cave caved in!" That's Vicky, at Paul's elbow.

"My grandfather was an *andarte*," says Paul.

Was he? I'm tongue-tied.

"That is, my father was adopted by his aunt. And it was her husband who was a member of the communist group who used this cave."

The next few minutes are a bit of a blur for me, but I take in enough. I learn much more on the walk back to Glikopigi, in the company of Paul and Holly. Holly knew that Paul was Anglo-Greek with family connections in the village but it was obvious she was now learning more surprising details. (Something else that became obvious during the walk was the strong attraction between her and Paul. No wonder Poor Niggle chose to go to the States).

By the time we reached the river after a rapid descent down the steep slope, we'd learnt that Paul's Greek family, although originally from Glikopigi, lived in Rumania in the late nineteenth, early twentieth century. A couple of brothers had a successful import-export business, dealing in olives, olive oil and wool. Paul's great grandfather inherited and married a Rumanian; they had two daughters and lived a good life in Budapest. Unfortunately, he and his wife got involved in the politics of the 1930s. They were both actively left-wing and campaigned against the fascists. In 1938 they disappeared.

"No-one here in Glikopigi ever knew what happened to them. The two daughters who were in their late teens came to live with their childless uncle and his wife. Ileana and Roxanne were grateful for their board and lodging but had to work hard for it. They had been living a life of comparative luxury in Budapest. Now they were herding goats. At least, Roxanne was, while Ileana did all the running around, taking in washing, working in the vegetable gardens below the village, carrying home wood from the hillsides and water from the spring."

I manage to ask a question. "I've been told that Ileana is still alive, but Roxanne fell in the gorge?"

"That's right. Ileana is still alive and Roxanne did fall to her death. She'd given birth to my father Andreas only months before that."

"Oh, is Roxanne the deaf and dumb grandmother you've talked about?" asks Holly. Now the path alongside the river has widened, I see that they are holding hands.

A disturbing thought has come to me. I hear again someone's remark about Ileana and Alex.

I'll dare the question.

"And Andreas's father? Who was that?"

"We never knew. Roxanne was a deaf mute. She spent a lot of time alone, looking after the goats during the summer months. She lived in a cave, about the same size as ours, but much further up the gorge. No-one ever went there; except for Telis and Ileana. Telis was a widower; he really needed his nieces' help. We wondered if a stray German had found her. The Germans used to check up on things in Tesserahori. It's not out of the question that a German, interested in plant-collecting perhaps ..."

His voice trails away. I breathe more easily. I didn't want to think of my father taking advantage of a young Greek girl who was deaf and dumb. I couldn't and wouldn't believe it. But on the other hand, a second world war plant-collecting Heinrich? No. A German if at all like Heinrich would be too honourable. A Nazi, then? I glance forward to take a close look at Paul's colouring. He has light brown hair. What about his eyes? I'll check at the next opportunity.

"Mind, Granny!"

Holly's voice brings me sharply back to the present moment, walking over twisted tree roots that make the path hazardous.

"What a story!" I exclaim. "I'd like to meet Ileana. Will you take me?"

Holly, it appears, has told Paul my reason for being in Glikopigi. He understands my keenness to meet someone who was alive in those war years.

"Certainly. What about you and Holly coming to lunch with us on Sunday?"

Yes! I see I've provided them with an extra reason to be together. He's a much more suitable partner for Holly than Poor Niggle.

II CHAPTER TEN

Heinrich is throwing bread to the ducks in a carefully systematic way. He regulates his throws so that the bigger ducks are competing for one chunk while he aims several smaller bits in the path of the more timorous ducks. He is quite absorbed in this. I'm not sure he's really listening to me, but he's still encouraging me to talk about my years in the estate agency. I can't think he's really interested. It all sounds so mundane.

We're sitting on the terrace of the fish restaurant. It overhangs the river, just a quarter of a mile from the bridge my father blew up. Such an ordinary road bridge, too. Heinrich left me to wander about on my own. But the gulf between the violent past and the placid normality of the present almost put the significance of the moment out of reach. I could see Heinrich's green car parked the far side of the bridge. There was not any other vehicle in sight. The road stretched across the plain ahead into the distance. After the bridge, the road wound up the hillside behind the fish restaurant. I strained to see into the past, yearning to make some kind of imaginative contact with my father. But – nothing. A blank.

Perhaps, I said, when I joined Heinrich in the restaurant, perhaps this is not the bridge. But I'm certain on a logical level that it is, from all I've learnt in Glikopigi. Perhaps I should believe in some sort of spiritual dimension to be able to connect at a deeper level with the past. I've actually felt a more dynamic connection with Alex when I've walked in what was countryside around Colebroke Farm. This is what I want to convey to Heinrich. The events and people of the past are running alongside us, could we but penetrate the mist that lies between us.

"Parallel universes?"

"If you like. I imagine us sitting in one tube train, which is the present. Alongside us, at the same station at any single moment, is the tube train which is the past."

Heinrich's quick glance in my direction is smiling and quizzical before he gets back to the job in hand: throwing bread pellets to ducks.

"Are the two trains going in opposite directions?" he asks. "And can you see from one train to the other without difficulty?"

"Same direction. And some people may see better than I can. There's too much mist and darkness in the way for me."

"Speaking for myself, I am one hundred per cent glad to be in the present without any glimpses of the past."

It now comes out. Heinrich has been in constant therapy for his childhood traumas. He was trapped under masonry for four days but at least his family house was in an outer suburb of the city and they escaped the fire balls.

I listen in silence and I'm still silent when he comes to the end of what he wanted to tell me.

He gets up, comes around the table to stand behind my chair. Then I feel the side of his face, his bristly beard, on my cheek, and his hands on my upper arms. I know there are tears in my eyes, which is ridiculous. He goes back to his chair.

"I didn't tell you this for your sympathy. I told you this because I trust you and I would like you to be present in my past. You see? We understand each other?"

I nod my head although I really don't understand what's going on. It feels momentous.

"Eat up. The fish is good. The ducks are hungry."

I have half a trout left on my plate, while Heinrich has only a thoroughly cleaned backbone and half a fish head on his.

He's seen what I'm thinking. "The cheeks and the eyes are delicious. The most tasty morsels of a trout."

"Well then, have mine too." I pass over my plate.

"Now. Tell me more about your life as an estate agent. I find it hard to imagine you wearing lipstick and a smart suit. And holding a clipboard."

"Is that what you think estate agents are like?

"I know very little about them. In Germany we don't buy and sell houses all the time like you Englanders."

"Well, it was something I really liked doing." I go on to describe how I first came to work in property.

Richard used to say that I joined his firm because of nostalgia for the land Joan's parents, my grandparents, sold to their neighbour, his father, Geoffrey Halbert. Possibly there's some truth in that. I did find it difficult to see all the houses being built around Colebrook Farm. But the main reason was that Richard, who I'd come to know during the school holidays – Scottish dancing, hunt balls – offered me the job as soon as I could do shorthand (badly) and typing (speed struggling to 50 words a minute).

"My mother's parents," I tell Heinrich, "ran quite a sizeable farm on the outskirts of Exeter. Joan, my mum, was living there when she married Alex. The farm was working well, despite wartime difficulties. It was after the war that things got difficult. Joan thought the decline was due to mismanagement. Her father sold twenty acres to Geoffrey Halbert who promptly sold it all to a developer. More land was sold off. Now you can't see any sign of the old hedges and fields that used to belong to Colebrook. Not a single oak tree left. The farmhouse itself – a thatched Devon longhouse, that's a traditional and very ancient kind of house – is surrounded by residential estates built over the last seventy years. My mother doesn't seem to mind at all. She says all the new houses brought life to the growing community. Colebrook is now the name of an Exeter suburb and not that far from the centre. Buses go past the farmhouse. There's a nursing home next door – her friend Sheena is in it and Joan can visit."

Heinrich interrupts his bread-throwing to ask how old Joan is and if she's still active.

"Well into her 90s. Still active – up to point. She's not going to ride her horse any longer, though, which is something she did until about ten years ago. She used to like to ride along the bridle ways that still exist up from the orchard of the farm to a wooded hill two or three miles away. I'm not sure but I think it has significance for her, from Alex's day, something she'd never admit. For her, it' s all about forgetting the past, and protecting the present – in other words, maintaining the comfort of the man she married soon after I was born. And the twins she produced a year later."

"Do you blame her? A young widow?"

"Not for that. But I do blame her for the way she erased as much trace of my father as she could."

There. I have never voiced this before. Not in so many words. Richard knew I didn't want to keep in touch with the twins and I never liked to visit Colebrook but neither he nor I understood the depth of my resentment towards my mother. I look across at Heinrich. He was a stranger until a few days ago, yet I'm talking to him at greater length than I've ever talked with anyone.

"I used to invite Joan, every so often, to our house for Sunday lunch." I realise, as I tell Heinrich this, that the Sunday lunch ritual ended when Joan could no longer drive. And that was many moons ago. Oh dear. Here I am, hunting for the ghost of my father, while neglecting my mother who's still alive.

I'll ask Holly to text John and pass a message to Joan. I don't want to phone her myself; I know how badly I would feel speaking to her. I'm out here, looking for the ghost of the husband she did her best to forget.

"John, one of the twins, and his wife live in the farmhouse. They keep an eye on Joan. She lives in the stables that were converted for her years ago."

"She is looked after. You can enjoy yourself here. More wine?"

We go on to talk about wine. Heinrich suggest that I meet him in the Rheinland in the autumn for a wine-tasting river trip. I smile but say nothing. I'll think about this later, on my own.

II CHAPTER ELEVEN

It's fixed. Paul has arranged that Holly and I will meet Ileana this coming Sunday. Meanwhile Heinrich has arranged the ravine walk with William and Kathy for today. Once again, boots on, stick in hand. This time, up the mountain rather down it.

Strange how fast my time here has become so full and colourful, so *peopled*. Before I arrived, Glikopigi was the name for the blank space in my life set aside for my hunt, without my having the slightest idea how I would conduct that hunt. All I could imagine ahead of time was finding the bridge and standing on the spot where my father was shot and killed. Well, I've found the bridge but I now realise that of course the bridge itself could not be the exact spot. He would have been escaping from the scene, as fast as he could, after the explosion. The Germans who opened fire on him would have needed a few minutes to react. He might have been two hundred yards away. Who have I met so far who was there with him? Yiannis. I shall return to talk with Yiannis. Perhaps he'll be willing and able to come with Heinrich and me to the area of the bridge. I could treat him to a trout lunch. Then he could lead me to the very spot. Yes, I shall put that plan in place.

Heinrich is ahead but not by much. The climb up the mountain is not straining my heart and lungs quite so cruelly. I've become fitter. I even have enough breath to chat a bit when we pause at the spring half-way up. We made a very early start – it's a whole day's trek. We have an exact time for the rendez-vous with William and Kathy at the head of the ravine. They'll have come up from Mikro Kipseli. We'll go down the ravine together. They'll return to Mikro by following the gorge to its start. We'll go down the gorge to the river's springs where Heinrich knows a path that will take us back to Glikopigi. Heinrich is in charge of timing, of course. It's good to be a passenger again.

Again? Was I a passenger with Richard? No, I don't think so. From the start of our marriage, he wanted me to be as independent as possible within the firm. When the children came along I developed a way of keeping my hand in as well as being a full-time mother. I advertised in Country Life as a house-matchmaker. Like today's personal shoppers, I shopped for homes in the west country for people who worked and lived abroad and were looking for a retirement property. Small beginnings when I was trawling the countryside with babies in tow, but I slowly built up my micro-agency within Halberts. "You're a natural," said Richard when the revenue I generated began to make a difference to our profit margins. "We should call the yacht *Matchmaker*." Those were the days, I think to myself sadly. They lasted until the crash in 2008. But – here I cheer myself up and escape these fruitless rat runs of thoughts -we were in any case gradually easing ourselves into retirement. Halberts had been swallowed up in a national chain, so we no longer had the same enthusiasm for our work.

"What about you?" I ask Heinrich who's filling his water bottle. I've responded enough to his prompts for life story. "I bet you still enjoy your work."

"Yes, I do – now that I am writing for students rather than teaching them."

It transpires that he's written four books, all about the flora and fauna of different habitats around the world. "For kids of 14 to 16. But who reads any longer? I am developing digital versions of the books with a friend."

The thought of Heinrich having a friend doesn't suit me. I realise I want him to be absolutely unconnected with anyone. Free as the wind. For my benefit.

He makes it more difficult when he adds something about 'she'. The friend is a she!

"I shall go on," I say, getting to my feet, grabbing my stick. "You'll overtake me in any case before we get to the ridge."

I know I'm experiencing the same feelings I had when I was a child. Resentment. Jealousy. And here I am, not just an adult but an old woman! And all because of someone I've only just met! What goes on in us humans? It's baffling.

I pause and let Heinrich catch up, which he does swiftly. "Okay?" he asks.

I turn and look at him. Our eyes are level as I'm placed slightly higher on the path. He has kind eyes – a kind expression – and all around us is a spectacular expanse of sky and the receding ridges of our own and other mountains. It's as if we are standing alone on the world's balcony.

"Yes, okay." It's actually marvellous.

William and Kathy have got to our meeting point first, a cairn of stones at the head of the ravine. William is carrying a metal detector that belonged to his father. It looks rusty and old-fashioned, but William says it still works.

"My dad was a magician with electronics. Before electricity came to Tesserahori, he rigged up solar panels connected to a bank of batteries and so we had – when we were there on holiday – electric light, a fridge, and a small cooker. Our neighbours were astonished."

Heinrich is interested. While the two men (gender differences!) talk about tracking and location depths, operating frequencies, and the reach of telescopic arms, Kathy and I confer about the food we've brought. She hopes we haven't doubled up on hard-boiled eggs. I say we are more likely to have too much cheese pie.

"No," she says, "I've made spinach pie. That's my speciality when we're here." She collects edible weeds from the mountainside.

We fall into talk about their London life. She goes off into a description of their work which I struggle to follow. Single words I understand – *bespoke, software*. It's just when they are threaded together that I lose track of the meaning. And Kathy uses lots of initials. What is ERP? I ask. Enterprise resource planning systems, she replies. "Mostly, though, we offer small scale sales and purchase order software."

She waits for a response. "You obviously keep at the cutting edge of things," I manage.

"No retirement for us, yet awhile," she answers. "What about you?"

I'm not going into my life again. I'm here to hunt for the sovereigns that were dropped with supplies and – most importantly - my father. He must have landed in this ravine. It's unlikely we'll find any trace of anything with Lenny's old metal detector. Kathy and I turn to the men.

"For your interest," Heinrich is saying in his lecturer voice, "the inventor of the first metal detector was the amazing Alexander Graham Bell, the inventor of the telephone."

Telecommunications, wireless operators, computer software designers – I'm from a different universe.

Heinrich expands on the information he's giving us. "An American president – I am sorry, I forget his name – it was in the late 1800s – was shot by an assassin but not killed outright. Bell quickly put together a kind of metal detector to locate the bullet. It was an electromagnetic device. The president died before he'd finished making it."

I'm afraid I find this funny. I imagine Bell in his workshop surrounded by gadgets, desperately fitting bits and pieces of metal and wires together while the White House staff hang around impatiently. I catch my explosion of laughter in the back of my nose. A snigger. It's not noticed as William and Heinrich are in earnest discussion.

"If I'm not mistaken, the first portable metal detector was invented by one of your compatriots." William's voice turns this from a statement into a question. I see them in armour charging towards each other, knights on horseback.

Heinrich is silent. No, he doesn't know this. Why would he?

William takes the field. "Yes, a Dr. Gerhard Fisher. He emigrated to America before the war and founded the Fisher Research Laboratory. I think in the early 1930s or maybe the late 1920s."

But now Heinrich comes back in. "Fisher, yes, I do know the name. He was originally from Dresden, I believe." I'm rooting for Heinrich and feel smug with his response. Dresden was his home town – maybe that's how he comes by this abstruse knowledge. "The Metalloscope was his invention, was it not?"

Though he's speaking English, I hear a thoroughly German and triumphant *Nicht war*. And what about metalloscope! Fantastic. Is William unseated? I'm afraid not.

"My father Lenny had one of the first M-scopes!" William is delighted to be able to say this.

And I don't even know how to make a Greek cheese pie, let alone which weeds are edible.

We set off, William leading. This is the fourth time he's searched the first section of the ravine. Below a certain point it becomes impossible. The drops between levels are too great. "The first time we brought a metal detector here was in 1953," he tells us. "I was a lad of seven. Dad had made the detector, putting together bits from god knows what. I think a vacuum cleaner handle had something to do with it. There were various trailing cables to a box with a huge battery which my mother had to carry. He was quite a magician."

His voice comes and goes as we follow behind, single file. The terrain is treacherous. There's a network of narrow but deep, dry, stream beds leading into the ravine. We jump from one patch of even ground to another, skirting the bigger rocks. As we descend, the sides of the ravine, which splits this shoulder of the mountain in two, draw closer until we reach a point where we can see down into the bed of the ravine. We could slither down to land on a smooth shelf of rock. Winter snow would pile up here. Heavy rain would wash any loose object down to the floor of the gorge, out of sight far below us. It reminds me of looking down the escalator of a London tube station but on a far larger scale. I think we're on a fool's errand if we want to find a single gold sovereign dating from the war years. But, for me, there's nothing foolish about the search. I *know* I'm close to my father. He was most definitely here.

William suggests we take a break before getting down into the ravine proper. "I'll roam around with the detector and you others spread out and hunt with your eyes and feet. Look in all the holes and crevices. We're not looking for loose coins. They'll be in a tin canister about the size of an old-fashioned milk churn."

"If the canister has rusted away – which is likely – then there will be loose coins." Heinrich is surely right about this.

"The main thing is to look for anything that doesn't belong here," says William.

Kathy, who has attended two previous searches, adds, "Bits of parachute silk or rope."

"Wouldn't material like that rot away to nothing?" That's my contribution.

"You never know. Caught in a hole, covered by undergrowth. Keep a sharp eye open."

We spread out.

Later

I'm absolutely shattered. I've just managed to have a shower and get myself to lie on the bed, like a medieval queen on her sarcophagus. My heels, rubbed raw by my boots, hurt like hell. My left big toe feels broken. My leg muscles ache. I have a penetrating pain behind my eyes. I'm ravenous, but I can't face getting up and meeting Heinrich as arranged at a table in the courtyard.

And all this for nothing.

We found not a glint of gold. Not a hint of rusty iron. Not a scrap of white material or rope. Nothing manmade was impressed on the landscape by the events of the second world war. In the gorge, in the ravine, Nature has been left to its own devices, season upon season, years upon years, centuries upon centuries.

That, I suppose, is as it should be.

Still, my father continues to exist in my imagination. And I still have the chance of standing on the spot where he was killed.

II CHAPTER TWELVE

This is like being part of a broad, swiftly flowing river. Voices and people, drink and food, are carrying me along, smiling happily at everyone and nothing. I can only follow a certain amount; that is, when someone turns towards me with something particular to say, more slowly, more carefully. This happens every now and again. The rest of the time I sit, eat, drink and listen. It's a wonderful feeling to be simply accepted and tolerated without having to do anything to earn it. Heinrich sits across the large square table and catches my eye every so often. Holly is on my right with Paul next door to her. There are about fifteen of us altogether – women, men and children of varying ages, from nought to ninety as the expression goes. Two of the middle-aged women come and go between the table in the courtyard and the kitchen, a separate, squat building attached to the main house. Ileana herself must well into her 90s. She, the matriarch of the tribe, sits in pride of place.

She is a striking-looking woman, with white hair swept up into a coil held in place with a large slide, the shape, pattern and colour of a peacock's spread tail. Her face is dark-skinned and heavily lined in a way that shows she has smiled a lot in her life and frowned less often. Her bone structure - cheekbones, jaw, forehead – is enviable. That's the view of someone with an indefinite, unmemorable face, or so I consider mine to be. She's wearing something velvety the colour of plums – a jacket? Embroidered? Edged with braid? People say that she and Nikos were a devoted couple, seldom apart. I expect she did wear black in the year after his death. But widow's black is no longer her choice. I can't look too hard, although my eyes are drawn to her frequently. There's something gypsy-like about her. Her eyes – dark brown, almost black – are bright and quick. Whenever her eyes meet mine, I feel a warm thrill go through me. She calls me Aleka, the feminine form of Alekos. I'm not sure if this is intentional or caused by the confusion of old age. It makes me feel within touching distance of my father.

Alex loved her. Of course he did. Who wouldn't. And who told me that? I've met so many people and been told so many things that I find it hard to sort out. Generally, the folk memory of Kapetan Alekos is of a heroic Englishman who gave his life for the village. The fact that the Germans retaliated has only been briefly mentioned. I'm relieved that it wasn't Glikopigi that was burnt down but a village to the north, known for its active resistance group and assumed to be responsible for the destruction of the bridge. The conversation is always swiftly pulled back to Alekos, the perfect English gentleman and soldier, making me feel so proud of him.

This Sunday lunch is a far bigger occasion than I'd expected. The reason is that family members have returned for next week's festival, the annunciation of the Virgin Mary on August 14th. Every room in the house is occupied – and it's clearly a big house. Paul – Pavlos in this setting - leans across Holly to fill me in every so often. I won't remember the names and relationships, but I get the picture in a rough way. Nikos and Ileana married soon after my father was shot. Then Ileana's sister – the deaf-mute Roxanne -surprised the family by appearing pregnant. When the baby was born, Ileana took over his care, Roxanne being thought incapable of it. He was christened Pavlos.

"My grandfather," says Paul. "You know the tradition of naming a child after a grandparent?"

"Ah. That explains why there are so many people with the same name."

I'm not sure when exactly Roxanne fell to her death but Ileana brought up Pavlos from babyhood. He was viewed as the first child of the family, the leader of the four she and Nikos went on to have. Present-day Pavlos names some people around the table; all part of this family or married into it. I am astonished by the way noise and excitement has taken over what started as an almost painfully stilted meal. The presence of three foreigners made the family self-conscious? That state didn't last long. I look across at Heinrich; even his forehead is flushed from the wine. Mine must be, too. One of the sons or nephews has been making sure no glass stays empty. I know I should leave just a little in the glass to delay the filling, but I forget to do this. Down it all goes.

It's the first time I've seen Heinrich without his cap. He's not completely bald but only a thin layer of hair covers his scalp. It's long enough at the back to gather in a pony tail but today he's left it loose. This suits him far better. He looks like a benign and distinguished Victorian. Had I any say in the matter, I'd encourage him to give up the cap and the pony tail and shave the beard.

He notices my attention and flashes a smile at me. Pointing to his nearly empty plate, he mouths "Good?"

It was a beef stew and it was exceptionally good. Someone - a mother, a cousin, an aunt – told me which of them was the cook. But I've given up trying to learn names.

Great smiling slices of water melon are now on the table. I wish I could enjoy a slice but, in some harbour or other when Richard and I got caught up in a similar celebration, I was fed forkful after forkful of the horribly watery, tasteless, red stuff. Each time I opened my mouth to say no, another chunk went in. I think this is called aversion therapy.

I tell Ileana this and she laughs, a deep throaty laugh like a smoker's. "You are funny, Aleka *mou*." My Aleka. I feel like a cat being stroked.

I'm sitting beside her. She pointed to a spare chair after the children had been allowed to leave the table and a few of the adults followed. I'm hoping she may be about to talk about my father.

"Your mother is still alive?" she asks. "We must be about the same age. Has she all her marbles?"

I let out a surprised laugh.

"Yes, I see you wonder how I know such an expression." She proceeds to talk about her childhood in Rumania before the second world war. Her family was clearly well off. They lived in Budapest. Ileana had an English governess. Her parents became embroiled in the politics of the time. They were anti-fascists, she explains. They were imprisoned, the two of them. "We never saw them again."

Nothing I can say is adequate.

Ileana talks English fluently but with a strong accent that seems to me a mixture of Rumanian and Greek sounds. She rolls her r's deep in her throat, and lengthens any adaptable vowels into long eee sounds.

"It was terrrreeeeble, the never knowing what happened to them. The brotherrrrr of my fatherrr" - but you must hear it in your own head, it's too hard to write – "brought Roxanne and me back to Greece and we had food and shelter. Not much love, though. Telis had never married and lived with his great-aunt, here, in this house." She waves a hand in a wide gesture, taking in the house, the courtyard, the outhouses. "Imagine. I was on the brink (brrreeeenk) of adulthood, I came from a bright city, and here I was. Surrounded by *goats*."

I thought she said ghosts before I understood she was referring to Telis's herd of animals.

"Telis found us useful. I helped great-aunt with the cooking and cleaning. I took in washing, as we had no money. Roxanne looked after the goats in the summer months, taking them to the gorge and guarding them against wolves and bears. Did Heinrich show you the cave she lived in, on your way back the other day from the ravine?" Rrrraveeeeen.

How is it that everyone in this village knows the movements of everyone else? I expect it's always been like this, but mobile phones make it easier. "No," I reply. "But he pointed it out." It was just a dark crease high above us on the gorge's cliff face as we drew near the springs. "He'd been there in the past, on a plant-collecting expedition."

Holly has been following our conversation and now moves to an empty chair the other side of Ileana. She wants to know if Roxanne's cave is like the one they're excavating. Ileana looks vague. "I suppose it might be," she answers after a pause. "But we weren't interested in the past at all, not even in what happened the year before. The present was too much of a struggle. Is history a luxury, do you think?" Heeestorrrreeee, luxurrrreeee, theeenk?

Paul joins in. "A necessity, I reckon. Surely the people who were fighting in your youth were obsessed with history. They were driven by the events of the past."

The three of them embark on a discussion. The only lesson of the past that I want to learn concerns the late summer of 1943. I excuse myself from the table to find the loo.

Ileana points the way to another small stone building beyond the kitchen. I would have liked to look inside the house but accept that this is easier. I'm relieved to open a door on a modern lavatory with shining white tiles and everything you could possibly need to wash and brush up. I feel ashamed that I expected something much more primitive, like some of the places we found on the islands, way back in the past.

When I rejoin the table, Ileana is tracing Holly's mouth, gently and slowly, with a finger. "The past can still be present, can't it," she murmurs. She looks up at me, in a questioning sort of way. "I wonder," she says. "Is it time? Shall I?"

Time for what? What on earth is coming?

"I don't suppose it will do any harm now." She turns to Paul. "I've never wanted to tell you this but since Nikos died, it has been on my mind, night and day."

I can feel Paul and Holly going as silent inside as I feel.

"Nikos was not the father of your grandfather Pavlos. You know that."

"He was good to me," puts in Paul hastily. "And you have always been my great granny even if you are my great grandaunt."

Ileana is talking over him. "Yes, Nikos was a good man. He always wanted to make things better in whatever way he could. He tried to be the father of Pavlos, in place of the unknown father."

Ileana paused for a moment to take a sip of water. "No one ever knew who that was. I have never told a soul."

Paul is clutching his glass of wine. I reach for mine. Holly puts a hand on my lap. We don't know what to expect, but we know that whatever it is will shake us.

"The father of Roxanne's baby was Aleko. Helen's father is Paul's great grandfather."

There's a stunned silence as the three of us take this in. Then our questions follow.

"Does that make Paul and me – *cousins*?" asks Holly.

I'm asking Ileana how she knows and if she knows for certain.

Paul is looking aghast.

Ileana holds her hands up. "You see? Is knowing the past a luxury or a necessity. I need a rest."

She can't be going to have a rest right now, leaving us with this new, undigested knowledge?

But she is. One of her daughters, about my age, comes close with a zimmer frame and helps Ileana away.

II CHAPTER THIRTEEN

I didn't sleep much last night. I kept going over what Ileana told us yesterday. Her sister – the deaf and dumb mute who lived in a cave in the gorge, looking after the family goats – had been *impregnated* by my father. That was the word that came to mind, a suitable one for an act which cannot have had any loving element. What a dreadful picture of my father this has created. Could Ileana tell me more that would soften it in some way? If my father had fallen for *Ileana*, rather than her sister, and a baby had resulted, a half-brother or sister for me – then I might have accepted this. I can see how irresistible she might have been for a young soldier, far from home, in wartime, in danger. But making Roxanne pregnant – taking advantage of a simple-minded country girl? It makes me feel sick.

I need to re-write history. How can I do that? I can't!

Michalakis has been hovering nearby, making sure his few guests have what they need for breakfast. Now he comes close and asks if anything is wrong. I look up at his kind face which is crumpled into an expression of concern. I can find no words to reply.

He pulls out a chair and sits down. "Is it not going so well?" he asks.

I'd like to be able to ask his advice. I'd like to be one of the daily problems I've watched him dealing with so calmly and speedily: phoning suppliers, seeing to guests' well-being, calming Maria in the kitchen. But I cannot let out the information that my granddaughter and Paul are cousins, even if at third remove, for this would put my father into the reviled position of the rapist of Roxanne, hitherto unknown. I'm overheating just to voice this in the privacy of my own head.

The sultry weather today does not help. Storm clouds have gathered on the horizon, above the last ridge of mountains that lie in Albania. If only it would rain ...

"Oh, I'm fine, fine," I say to Michalakis. The words come out in a strangulated way that sounds anything but fine.

"I know what you need," says Michalakis. "You were drinking Ileana's wine, so you need a shot of tsipouro. After that you will go to visit Anna-Maria. No-one visits Anna-Maria without feeling much better as a result."

I haven't heard this name before. My curiosity does make feel immediately better. Michalakis describes her as the Dutch wife of a local man. They live in Athens but come here at holiday times. "She will tell you anything you need to know about the war years. She's a historian. She has written books in English about the area during the German war and the bad times that followed." Her husband is the psychiatrist son of one of the *andartes* who Alex would have known.

I'm on my way as soon as I finish breakfast.

Anna-Maria is in her courtyard coming towards the entrance as I enter. Michalakis has obviously phoned her on his mobile, to give advance notice of my visit.

She's a thin, middle-aged woman with brownish-blonde hair piled on top of her head in a hurried, haphazard way. Her greeting is brisk but warm enough. She guides me to a wrought-iron table in the courtyard and gestures to me to sit down on one of the two iron chairs. She'll bring me coffee, she says; how do I like it? *Metrio*, medium. No, I'm not to follow her into the kitchen. I must just sit and watch the mother cat and kittens playing in the courtyard.

As Anna Maria opens a fly-screened door onto a separate building, a fierce altercation is momentarily audible before the door bangs shut. The same sounds emerge when she returns with a tray of coffee and water. She must have noticed my expression for she immediately supplies an explanation

"My mother-in-law and her sister. Always they do this. Cats fighting."

It doesn't come out at once but the thing that most interests me immediately is not information about the war years or the civil war but the fact that the house is neatly split in two. The line of division runs through the middle of the kitchen. This is extraordinary. Mother-in-law has one side of the kitchen. Her sister, the other. They never cross the invisible line. They never converse. They fling biting remarks into the air to be heard on the other side of the line. The battle, says Anna, keeps them going. Without it, they would die.

The irony of this, and the way she tells it, delights us both. It is possible, we agree, to laugh at what is in reality distressing. The bitter quarrel acted out in the actual fabric of the house makes their short visits from Athens very awkward. Their children never come. This eccentric situation is the result of a will two generations ago, the material for an unsolvable family quarrel.

"The micro is in the macro," says Anna-Maria and we start thinking of all the divisions in the world, piling them up one on top of the other in any order of place and time. The Berlin Wall, North and South Korea, the Great Schism of 1054 (Anna-

Maria's contribution of course) when Roman Catholic church parted company with the Eastern Orthodox church, the Remain and the Leave of Brexit chaos (mine), Ulster and Eire, Protestants and Catholics, Sunnis and Shiites, black citizens and white policemen, Rohingya Muslims and Buddhists in Myanmar, Tutsis and Hutus ... the list goes on and on.

"I like to think in terms of the fundamental laws of nature," says Anna-Maria, leaning forward to take a grip on the free-wheeling conversation "Forgive me if my English is not so good to express what I think. You know the big bang?" She demonstrates with her hands. "Everything flew apart, then started joining together. That's how it has to be. A split has to be followed by a union. You see? Nothing goes on splitting for ever, nor stay together for ever. The smaller elements need to join; then they need to – pouff! - go in different directions. Think about it. Everything obeys this law. It's like a pulse, in and out. You'll start noticing. You can't breathe in without breathing out. We are creatures of universal laws. It's no surprise when people emphasise their differences, even down to drawing lines through kitchens."

I look at her doubtfully. I envy her her certainty.

"You should talk with Yiannis," she says when our conversation has gone back to the war years. "My husband's father was Odysseas, who was part of the *andartes* resistance group. So was Yiannis. I know he - that is, Yiannis - actually saw your father shot."

I'm knocked back by this. "I have met him and his wife. Poppy. But he didn't let on he actually saw what happened."

"It would be too difficult."

"Difficult?"

"He lives here, in this village."

I'm not sure what she means by this. I take a sip of coffee while I think about it. She continues.

"As this house demonstrates, even in peacetime there are rivalries, antagonisms. And the same holds true within a single individual, doesn't it. I know I am often torn between my good side and my bad. Aren't you?"

True.

"Until we can see ourselves clearly and admit our own faults, then there is no hope of reconciliation."

She is about to continue when there's a penetrating yowl. We turn to see the mother cat springing to her feet, tossing kittens right and left. She arches her back and hisses in the direction of the courtyard wall. A rival cat must have appeared but there's no sign. She's looking towards the mountain which is visible above the lych gate, although partly hidden by village cherry trees in the immediate foreground. I hear a strange, deep rumble. Thunder? No, it doesn't come from the sky. It's more like a London tube train passing under our feet. The ground is no longer stable. The coffee cups rattle. The table tips and falls as I try to grab it. There's nowhere safe to be. I feel sick in the pit of my stomach. Anna Maria takes hold of my wrist and pulls me towards the lych gate, both of us staggering like drunks. This strikes me as the wrong place to be. The slabs of stone on the doorway's roof are tumbling, one by one to the ground. I feel as though I'm in a lift shifting between floors, not coming to rest. My brain has begun to work again. This is an earthquake and it shows no sign of stopping. A roar from the direction of the mountain. Something has come loose up there and is falling. My mind flies to Holly and the cave. She's out there.

Later

I stayed with Anna-Maria and helped her clear up the broken coffee cups and set a number of fallen flower pots to rights. She was very matter-of-fact about the earthquake. They have them often enough in Greece, she said, and this one wasn't at all bad. She understood my concern for Holly and told me that the cave had been almost destroyed in a previous *seismos*, a long time ago. Odysseas used to talk about it, her husband's father.

I didn't find that comforting at all and left as soon as I felt the ground would take my weight without shifting. I can tell you it's a most disturbing feeling when it doesn't.

Still, all is normal now and I'm back home at the guest house. Michalakis and Maria are sweeping up debris and getting the tables and chairs upright and in place again. They tell me that a big rock fell from the mountain and came to rest in a stable belonging to what they call Telis's house, which I know is Ileana's. Everyone standing around talking it all over agrees that it's a miracle it didn't land on the house itself. I gather that the stable lies a little way outside the village, on the way to the cave.

"What cave?" I ask quickly when I can make myself heard.

The answer goes some way to relieve my anxiety. No, not the archaeologists' cave but Telis's. Again, I know this is as good as saying Roxanne's, and it must be the one where .... But I can't go on with that thought. I ask instead if anyone has heard from the archaeologists.

"Are they all right?"

The answer is yes, they are and they are on their way back to the village.

Later

In fact, much later. Holly came to find me after she and the others had gone back to the hostel and washed and changed. She told me what happened.

They'd been working at the cave as usual when they heard rumblings which she thought was thunder. Paul had experienced an earthquake before and took immediate action. He got the team outside and up the hill to a smooth table of rock where the land flattened out above the little chapel.

"He wanted to get us into the chapel. He said it's safe under archways."

That was why, I thought to myself, Anna-Maria dragged me to the lych-gate.

"But the 'quake started before we got there. Paul was so calm!" Holly's eyes looked bigger and bluer than ever. I could see how much she's in love with him.

My mind sheered off into questions of cousinship. How does it work with generations? Are Paul and Holly first cousins three times removed? Or third cousins? And would it matter if they married and had children? I knew it was absurd to be thinking of anything as indefinite and as futuristic as this and I brought my attention back to the present. Holly was full of excitement, wanting to tell me every detail. She could hardly get the words out fast enough. .

"Then we saw this bloody great lump which had come adrift from the mountain and it was falling. We could hardly bear to watch because it seemed to making straight for Paul's family house, Ileana's, at the top of the village but actually it was coming down further towards the gorge, in fact it went into the gorge and we lost it from view. Wasn't it a horrible feeling, not knowing where to run to, no firm ground anywhere – but Paul was wonderful. He kept saying it would be over very soon. When it did eventually stop, it didn't feel like it was very soon. Paul said it only lasted a minute and a half minute. Incredible! He'd timed it on his phone. So cool! He made us stay where we were for a while, as a precaution. Then we went back down to the cave. We could hardly believe our eyes! A big piece of land had simply slid away. It was like a giant dentist had taken a huge great molar out of an enormous mouth. The side of the cave had disappeared and left in its place ... wait for it, granny!"

Holly can only just wait herself. Her eyes are on me as she breathes the word.

"TREASURE!"

"Heavens above!"

"Gold coins! Hundreds of gold coins! Spilling out of a tin can sort of thing, spilling down the mountainside, a stream of gold coins! And gunpowder, or at any rate something white and powdery which we guessed was gunpowder, and guns and boxes of bullets and socks and jars of Marmite and Bovril! Can you believe it? All that gold! Isn't it amazing luck."

II CHAPTER FOURTEEN

A noisy party developed later in the day when Paul and the team joined Holly and me at a table in the guesthouse courtyard. People gathered around to hear about the find, to tell their own stories of the morning's earthquake, to relate anecdotes from the war years as well as present day tales of sovereigns selling for huge sums in Athens. They talked of people who'd hoarded Turkish currency under their beds since the days of the Pasha in Yannina – worthless now! The sovereigns must be converted into euros as soon as possible. But gold holds its value! We must hold on to it. Who does it belong to? Who will benefit from the find? Everyone had a view. Arguments arose over the best course of action. The guns should be handed in to the police. Or to the army. Or shared out and hidden in the village. You never know what will happen in the future. The dynamite ---- well, what about that? It is probably worthless after all these years. No, dynamite doesn't lose its strength. It could be very useful for blasting rocks away for the foundations of new hotels. And what about those slippery things in the river? Shh. Laughter.

All agreed that it wasn't going to be easy to decide what to do with the treasure trove but they were clearly going to have a high old time discussing it. Bottles of beer mounted up on the table. Maria and Michalakis came and went from the kitchen, bringing plates of salad and bread. Heinrich turned up – in fact, most of the able-bodied and loud-voiced in the village turned up. Heinrich leaned over the back of my chair and kissed my forehead. Did he intend to? Did I like it? Did Holly notice?

"Perhaps this is a matter for your mayor and community council?" he suggested to the gathering but no-one listened.

I slipped away after a while, full to overflowing with my own thoughts. I needed to plan the next step in my personal treasure hunt. I lay on my bed in the late afternoon heat and fell into a half-sleep. I saw Richard very clearly. I put him in the courtyard, standing behind the full to overflowing table. He'd have loved the scene. He would have wickedly encouraged the fantasies of what the haul could bring the village. You could build a swimming pool; a heated spa; give an annual scholarship to the children for travel and education abroad. I listened to his ideas but I couldn't recall the sound of his voice. This saddened me. I also felt guilty that I'd been neglecting him. My thoughts became a nightmare, from which I've only just woken up.

Too much beer at midday. It brought shotguns, explosions, dead bodies, chases and, worst of all, sink holes – bottomless pits in the mountain plateau which appeared beneath my feet and down which I fell and fell without ever reaching the bottom. I need to wash this nightmare away. I will get up, have another shower, a cup of tea, find Heinrich, visit Yiannis with him, and arrange our trip to the fish restaurant.

Three days later

I'm sitting opposite both Heinrich and Yiannis. Below me on my right, the river runs in green and blue frills and furbelows towards the bridge. After our trout meal, we'll cross the bridge to the spot where my father fell. Yiannis is confident he will find it exactly. I am trembling, in the way I used to do as a teenager at dances. I try and concentrate on what Yiannis is talking about.

While not actually the mayor himself any longer, after all, he's in his 90s, he still has much influence. He is telling us his views on the gold. Communal ownership is the only answer, he says. It had been dropped for all the resistance groups, not just the ones of Glikopigi. If Nikos were still alive, he'd be so pleased. He was forever trying to bring all the villages together, and he would certainly advocate this course of action.

Yiannis spreads his hands dramatically. "The mountain has opened up and delivered this opportunity to us. Scholarships for the next generation, yes, but first of all, a communal feast. *Etsi, prepei na'nai.*" That's how it must be. It sounds wonderfully decided and final. I believe Yiannis. He's that sort of person. He speaks fast but clearly and I can follow most of what he says. Heinrich supplies some translation when he notices I'm lost. Occasionally, Yiannis forgets what he's saying in the middle of a sentence, or the words get lost in forkfuls of trout being directed underneath his drooping, white moustache into his mouth. Today he has put on a clean white shirt and a striped blue and white tie. His trousers no longer fit him, he's lost weight, and holds them up with a wide leather belt. He wears stout leather hiking boots. Somewhere within this elderly, white-haired figure is the young man who brought freshly shot game to the cave to roast over the fire, and went with Lenny to the spot above the cave to transmit messages to Cairo.

"The feast will mark the end of the very many years during which we've lived with the aftermath of the civil war. You two foreigners can have no idea what we went through, and it's best you should not know. But, my dear Eleni, you've come all this way to learn about your father and you should know what happened."

I experience again the queasy feeling I had in my nightmare, of falling down a sink hole.

"Ileana has told you, hasn't she, that Kapetan Alekos fathered Roxanne's baby. She never told Nikos this. He remained ignorant of the facts. Now Ileana must remain ignorant of the things I shall tell you this afternoon. Please promise me this."

Heinrich is looking at me uncertainly. Does he think I shouldn't promise not to pass on something of which I know nothing as yet?

I search Yiannis's expression.

"I can't tell you unless you promise," he says with urgency. "I've kept silent about this all my life, and that's been hard. I won't have Ileana's trust thoughtlessly broken now."

I cannot help but promise. Refusing to learn what Yiannis can tell me would make my pursuit of truth worthless. I've always held that, unless we can face the truth in any given situation, we can never learn from our experience.

"I promise, certainly I promise."

"Good. Then when we are ready to go, let's go."

Next day

I'm slowly assimilating what I learnt by remembering how I leant it.

The three of us crossed the bridge but Heinrich stayed behind. He realised that this was going to be an emotional moment. But actually, by now, I was feeling as calm as I might be, if I was simply going to the dentist. Apprehensive, but not unduly so. Now the moment had come, the point of my journey, it seemed somehow mundane. A tour bus was holding up a truck which carried a bleating sheep. Heinrich was leaning against the iron railing of the bridge, watching our progress. There was something reassuring about the way he slowly raised his right hand in my direction.

Yiannis, a bent figure a few yards ahead of me, used his stick not so much for support but as a kind of metal detector. He prodded the ground and paused every now and again to look around and take his bearings. It wasn't long before he was satisfied that he'd found the exact spot.

"Here," he said. "It was here that your father fell. I was watching from our escape route up the mountain from that boulder over there." He waved his stick towards the rock and scrub-covered mountainside that rose steeply from the plain. "He was running fast from the bridge. He'd nearly crossed the open ground when he was shot. I saw him stagger, he was lit up by the flames of the explosion. Here. Right here he fell."

I looked for the boulder rather than turn my attention to the ground at our feet. It lay about 300 yards away from the bridge. The land was clear of bushes. Just dried thistles and grass at this time of year. A clear dash for it.

"Your father had set off the detonator. I wanted to do it but he wouldn't let me. I should have done it, as I was a faster runner. But it wouldn't have made any difference. Because it wasn't the Germans who killed him."

The landscape is starting to make me dizzy as I turn from the boulder to the bridge, from the bridge to the boulder and then to the gritty earth at my feet. I tell myself that my father died here. I feel remote. It really doesn't matter where, when or how you die. You just die and then you are no more. People say they want to die in their own bed with their loved ones around them. Loved ones! There's something sickly about the term. Who's deciding who loves whom and how much? I don't feel I've ever loved anyone enough. Alex was profligate. Selfish, too. He left my mother to come here on a fool's errand. What a terrible waste of a young man's life! My father robbed me of a father.

Then I hear the echo of Yiannis's words in my head. It wasn't the Germans who killed him.

Then who was it?

Yiannis has supplied the answer. It was Nikos.

Yiannis takes my hand and leads me across the stony earth to the boulder. He tells me that he knew Alex and Ileana were lovers. He often saw them together, down by the river, standing close, arms entwined. They used the chapel for love-making. He'd seen them go in and come out after half an hour, putting their clothes to rights, looking guiltily around – yet not seeing his watchful eyes. There was a look-out point close to Lenny's transmitter position. He was used to stalking and not being seen.

While Yiannis talks, I hunt around in my mind, calling up what I thought I knew, re-arranging scraps of information. Nikos, Ileana's husband who she loved, "such a good man", killed my father through jealousy, in calculated revenge. My father and Roxanne were lovers. My father and Ileana were lovers.

I push past Yiannis and bring up my lunch on a bush of sage.

Slowly, I make my way back to Heinrich on the bridge.

I feel devoid of emotion, scraped clean.

Richard. My father. Each as dead as the other.

Better never to love than love and lose.

II CHAPTER FIFTEEN

Better never to love than to love and lose.

That was my feeling last week. Now I'm home in England and I'm aware the bald statement no longer feels true.

I'm on my way from Sunday lunch with Rachel and family to see Joan at Colebrook. I'm driving down the motorway to Exeter. The trees in the verges are beginning to show autumn colours; it's been such a dry summer, everyone says the same thing. The reservoirs are almost empty. When will it rain? Caravans and motor homes travelling north stack up. On my side, there is the usual traffic: single-drivers in the fast lane while I and others like me juggle for space in the middle and inner lane, as we weave past colossal HGVs, their sides flapping.

When I was a child at Colebrook and couldn't sleep, I used to attempt a trick of the mind. I wanted to leave my body and travel to infinite time and space, imagining in detail each step of the way. I'd see myself in my striped pyjamas, cast-offs from John who'd outgrown them although he was a couple of years younger than me. I'd take a last look down at my body in its hollow on the mattress under the feather eiderdown, before I lifted up through the ceiling with its familiar pattern of cracks around the hanging central light inside its fringed, sepia-coloured shade, to whizz through the attic, under its creaking beams and up through the sneeze-inducing thatch. Once above the thatch, I'd be out into the night. Below me, I'd see the farm laid out in the way the twins I recreated farms with model animals –made of textured metal, painted cream for the sheep, brown and white for the cows and calves, pink for the pigs, cold and rough to touch but oh so real. I'd try not to get waylaid by thoughts such as how cross I'd been when Janet had used up all the sheep leaving me with an empty pen. I left these distractions behind as I hurtled up, leaving the world behind, to pass the moon and head for the stars. I'd urge my mind to imagine going on and on for ever, space and time with no end. This is where I'd probably fall asleep.

The sound of a horn brings me sharply back to the motorway. *Concentrate.*

We measure our lives in lengths of time. Such and such happened then, on that day, in that year. But what about measuring our lives in emotions? I've been away from home a bare three weeks, but emotionally I've been away a lifetime.

Rachel gave me my favourite lunch: avocado salad with slices of prosciutto. It was lovely to be just the two of us – quite rare nowadays as she's busy at work and when she's at home, the house is full of her children and now grandchildren. She wanted to hear about Holly, the earthquake, but most importantly about Paul. She'd first heard his name six months previously. His name cropped up in text messages more frequently than Nigel's.

"Poor Niggle," we said together.

"Paul is just the right sort of man for Holly," I said, preparing to launch into the Alex story. "He keeps her firmly tethered to the ground."

I'd said nothing on the phone from Glikopigi about what I'd learnt there. Now I was about to tell Rachel about her grandfather. How would I put it and how would she take it? That was my worry.

In the end, I was able to choose a form of words that neither exonerated Alex nor disparaged him. Rachel – typically – was more concerned about the effect of the relevation on me rather than on her.

"I'm getting used to it," I said. "It was a shock to begin with."

"From hero to what? What's a male hussy?"

"It was wartime," I said. "And he did love Joan."

In my bag I have letters to prove it, which I'm taking to show Joan.

"I would have liked to have a grandfather," Rachel admitted.

I had never thought of Alex's absence in her terms, being far too engrossed in my own response.

When she was a child, we hardly ever visited Colebrook to see Joan and Thomas. I am beginning to realise how my distance from them was down to my attitude. Did I need an explanation for my feeling of absence? Did I *need* to feel left out? Was it time to forgive my father for getting shot, even though I could now blame him for the behaviour that led to his death? Can one go on learning about oneself, all through life?

As we finished our salad, I knew I must now turn to the consequence of the Alex story on Holly and Paul's relationship. I described what I'd learnt from Ileana.

"Crumbs!" exclaimed Rachel. "What does it mean? Are they cousins? Does it matter?" That was my own first response.

"Not cousins. Closer than that. Let's start with me. I and Roxanne's baby are half-brother and sister. That's the first Paul who Ileana adopted. The tradition in Greece is to name the son after his grandfather. So Holly's Paul is the grandson of Pavlos, my half-brother. They share a great grandfather in Alex."

Rachel said she needed to draw a family tree. She looked as though she was enjoying the revelation. She said she'd never taken to Nigel but Paul had impressed her, the one time Holly brought him home.

"That was before she went out to Greece on this dig. I thought he was fantastic. Fearfully good-looking, kind and intelligent. I'd go for him."

"Yes. As an Anglo-Greek he comes across as a combination of all the best bits of each nation. But we don't *know* him, do we?"

I'm aware that I'm going to be cautious in the future about the assumptions I make about people. Appearances count for nothing. At the same time, I can't resist feeling that I meet my father when I see Paul.

"You know how our mouths are alike? Yours, mine and Holly's? Well, it may be pure imagination but I feel that I'm seeing my father when I look at Paul. They're about the same age, too. I mean, Paul's the age Alex had reached."

"Shame he died so young."

"Many did."

Joan and Ileana are both in their 90s and still alive and well. They are both alert in their minds. Not like poor Poppy, Yiannis's wife. Or Joan's friend in a home.

Home --- I'm driving towards my first home. I've had many since. Not like the Greeks who generally have one home, one house for life. Or used to, at any rate.

Richard and I had a good life together. The best bits were in Greece. But I must remember the way I loved being at home in Colebrook. Going home calendars started to be made at school as soon as the term began. I was ten when I left home for school.

I was five when I first learnt that Thomas was not my father.

They should have told me from the very start.

Off the motorway, the new road layouts confuse me for a moment and I have to go round a roundabout three times before I understand which way to go. So many changes so fast in the outskirts of Exeter. What used to be outskirts. Now estate upon estate of new houses. Where do all the people come from? What a ridiculous amount of land we humans take up. A cement planet any moment. But we won't last. A failing species.

This won't do. I mustn't have a long face for Joan.

Ah, Pinhoe. I recognise a newsagent. Now off on the Beacon Heath road.

Gone wrong. Turn off. Three point turn in the forecourt of Laburnum Avenue Rest Home. Is this where Joan's friend lives out her days, staring into space?

Now I'm on the right track. That's the estate built in the 1960s on two of Colebrook fields, Home Acre and Long Mead. The developers took some of the field names. Richard, even though we profited from the business of development, used to rant about the misappropriation of rural names: *Heathfield, Green Meadows, Orchard Lea.*

Now I am passing the orchard, the real orchard of Colebrook. It still exists, the trees red with cider apples. I turn in and park in the house's forecourt, which is where the milking parlour once stood. Straight ahead is Colebrook Stables, where Joan lives – the stable being a 1960s conversion, its name as inappropriate as any of the names of the roads around. Instead of five stalls with a cobbled floor beneath the feet of five horses, The Stables is a well-built and comfortable three-bedroomed home. If I was writing the brochure, I'd described it as having all the conveniences of the 21st century presented with old-world charm. There's a newly laid floor of Trevatine tiles from Italy. Or are they porcelain from China? I know there was quite a to-do when Joan had to move back into the farmhouse while the new floor was laid, not that long ago.

"*Carpet*, what's wrong with carpet. Expense for the sake of expense, if you ask me."

Spilt tea doesn't mark a tiled floor, but none of us say this.

She's sitting as usual in her chair by the window that looks over the square of lawn to the monkey puzzle tree and, beyond that, the orchard.

"Has Turner cut the grass? It's looking far too long."

She's not blind but her eyesight is failing. She's also rather deaf but won't wear hearing aids. *Blasted* things.

"Who's that? Is that John?"

"No, it's Helen."

"Oh, Helen." Toneless. Disappointed? Yet she sees John every day. He comes in at six o'clock to share a sherry and news of the day. I come in once every two months. I can't expect immediate recognition and a warm reception.

"Helen. Yes. Helen." It's as though she's reminding herself of something not essential. I might be on a par with the answer to where she last put her specs. This is her usual opening gambit.

She stirs in her chair, plucking at the tartan rug tucked around her legs. "Have we had tea?"

"I'll make it in a moment."

"Don't put sugar in."

"I never do."

"Come and sit close."

That's an unusual invitation.

"Helen. Yes, you are the daughter of Alex and me."

That's more unusual.

"You've been away in Greece. You went to see where Alex fell."

This is most unusual. So surprising in fact that I'm speechless. Not only has she mentioned my father, she's knows where I've been and why. I had no idea she'd taken in the purpose of my trip.

"So tell me. What did you find?"

The blue exercise book, found in a tin revealed by the landslip at the cave, is in my handbag. I thought I would lead gently up to it, but I've been hi-jacked.

"Something amazing," I tell her.

I shall hand it over to Joan, the right recipient, although the name *Ileana* is written in flowing Greek letters on the cover's nameplate. Inside there are pages of diagrams which I guess are ideas about the placing of the explosives on the bridge. But the most riveting pages are the ones on which Alex drafted letters home. There are many beginnings which peter out.

I sit close to Joan so that she can hear. "*My dearest darling Joan,*" I read but my voice cracks.

"Come along now," says Joan briskly, as she often did when I went into a dream as a child. Her tone of voice braces me and I continue to read.

It's amazing to think we were together not that long ago.

Or is it Richard's voice I hear?

First I must tell you … I can just read the words beneath the scratchings-out: *…what's brought me to this sorry pass.* In its place, he wrote *how much I love you.*

The words look hazy as I read them aloud and the realisation hits me. From all I learnt in Glikopigi, my father has become a living human soul, someone I could know and love, and now have well and truly lost. The lines in Tennyson's *In Memoriam* are the ones I should remember.

> *Tis better to have loved and lost*
> *Than never to have loved at all.*

I bend my head close to Joan's and let our cheeks wipe away each other's tears.

End

OTHER WORK BY SUSAN BARRETT, 1968 to 2019

Novels
JAM TODAY Michael Joseph ISBN 7181 0664 4
MOSES Michael Joseph ISBN 7181 0760 8
NOAH'S ARK Michael Joseph ISBN 7181 0892 2
PRIVATE VIEW Michael Joseph ISBN 7181 1036 6
RUBBISH Michael Joseph ISBN 7181 1288 1
THE BEACON Hamish Hamilton 0-312-07038-1
STEPHEN AND VIOLET Collins ISBN 0-00-223337-1
MAKING A DIFFERENCE Trafford ISBN 1-4251-1004-5
WHITE LIES Amazon ISBN 13-978-1536806847
A HOME FROM HOME Amazon ISBN 978 1537014838

Non fiction
TRAVELS WITH A WILDLIFE ARTIST
The living landscape of Greece, by Peter and Susan Barrett
Harrap-Columbus ISBN 0-86287285-5
ALIVE IN WORLD WAR TWO, The Cousins' Chronicle
Family letters exchanged during WW2
ISBN 9781537566030
THE GARDEN OF THE GRANDFATHER,
LIFE IN GREECE IN THE 1960s by Peter and Susan Barrett
Pencross Books ISBN 978– 1- 9996480-0-8
Illustrated with over 200 sketches and photographs
Also:
Natural history and children's books with Peter Barrett, published worldwide.

Many of these titles are also available as ebooks.
For more information, please visit https://susanbarrettwriter.com

Printed in Great Britain
by Amazon

44306283R00097